THE GUN

Also by Fuminori Nakamura

The Thief
Evil and the Mask
Last Winter We Parted

THE GUN

FUMINORI
NAKAMURA

Translated from the Japanese by Allison Markin Powell

SOHO

Jū © 2003 Fuminori Nakamura. All rights reserved.

First published in Japan in 2003 by
KAWADE SHOBO SHINSHA Ltd. Publishers.
Translation copyright © 2015 by Allison Markin Powell

First published in English in 2015 by
Soho Press
853 Broadway
New York, NY 10003

Library of Congress Cataloging-in-Publication Data

Nakamura, Fuminori, 1977–
[Ju. English]
The gun / Fuminori Nakamura ; translated by Allison Markin Powell.

ISBN 978-1-61695-590-8
eISBN 978-1-61695-591-5

1. College students—Japan—Fiction. 2. Firearms and crime—Fiction.
I. Powell, Allison Markin, translator. II. Title.
PL873.5.A339J8313 2016
895.63'6—dc23   2015028466

Interior design by Janine Agro, Soho Press, Inc.

Printed in the United States of America

10 9 8 7 6 5 4 3 2 1

So because thou art lukewarm, and neither hot nor cold, I will spew thee out of my mouth.

—Revelation, 3:16

Author's Note

The Thief, Evil and the Mask, and *Last Winter, We Parted* are my novels that have been translated into English to date. *The Gun* was written long before any of those books. It first appeared in a Japanese literary magazine in 2002, and the following year it was published in hardcover as my debut. I am delighted to see this long-ago novel of mine retroactively translated into English. My deepest gratitude to everyone who has been involved in the process, and to all those kind enough to read it.

Fuminori Nakamura

August 1, 2015

後書き

僕の小説は、これまで「スリ」「悪と仮面のルール」「去年
の冬、きみと別れ」と英訳されていますが、この小説は、
それらの作品よりもずっと前、2002年に日本の文芸誌に
掲載され、翌年単行本として刊行された僕のデビュー作に
なります。このように昔の僕の小説も遡って英訳されたことを、
とても嬉しく思っています。関係者の皆様、そして読んで
くれた全ての人達に深く感謝します。

2015年　8月1日　中村文則

1

LAST NIGHT, I found a gun. Or you could say I stole it, I'm not really sure. I've never seen something so beautiful, or that feels so right in my hand. I didn't have much interest in guns before, but the moment I saw it, all I could think about was making it mine.

It was raining last night. The kind of rain that seems like it will never stop, that falls at an angle, so even if you use an umbrella you still get soaked. I had been out walking around in it—if I had to say what time, it was about eleven at night. The relentlessness of the rain seemed to symbolize my own melancholy, and although from the knee down I was sopping wet and cold and couldn't wait to get out of it, for whatever reason I made no effort to head back home to my apartment. I really can't say why I kept walking around outside. I guess for no reason other than I just felt like walking, and I had no desire to go back to my own place. My actions were often motivated by such vague justifications. With no real plan, I changed course, passing through a street lined with darkened shops and along a side street that bordered a small park. I remember clearly that there was a small cat under a parked white van. The cat was staring at me. Come to think of it, this wasn't the only time a cat was watching me before something major happened. I didn't really register it at that moment, but now it seems like it might have been a forewarning.

I went over the railway tracks at a crossing, and passed through a warren of streets. Water had collected and was dripping down off of the edge of the roof of an old apartment building, falling persistently and loudly on broken pieces of prefab that were lying around. It was that sound, more than being pelted by the rain, that prompted me to think I ought to get back home soon.

In my mind, I pictured myself hurrying home, taking a shower, and changing into dry clothes. Yet I continued my aimless wandering with no end in sight. No matter how often I think about it, I can't seem to attach any specific meaning to my actions at that time. But then, it really wasn't all that unusual for me. On rare occasions, I would let things happen that were—I don't know—the opposite of what I wanted to do. Soaking wet and still nursing my melancholy thoughts, I kept walking.

Despite all this, I still take pleasure in the choice I made that night. I hardly ever used to evaluate my own past actions. I really didn't make a habit of thinking too hard about right and wrong, or about the consequences that arose from either. But I feel something akin to gratitude for what I did that night. Had I simply gone back to my apartment, I wouldn't have the gun in my hands now. In contrast, when I think about the possibility of never having had the gun, I am seized with a vague terror. Maybe it's wrong to think that, since it wasn't mine to begin with.

The next thing I did was buy a can of coffee from a vending machine. I wasn't thirsty, but I often drink coffee while I'm walking, so I bought it out of habit, more or less. I flipped the tab and took a sip as I stepped carefully to avoid the puddles that had formed on the asphalt. The sky was overcast with heavy gray clouds—neither the moon nor the stars were visible. There was a chill in the air—the rain had banished any trace of warmth from earlier in the day.

I continued to wander. Literally wandering; like I said before, I had no destination. I drank the canned coffee as I listened to the sound of the rain, and after I finished the coffee, I lit a cigarette. I passed through another warren of streets lined on either side with residences, and emerged onto a wide avenue. Cars sped along right beside me, sending up spray, not a single one slowing down as it passed. Needless to say, I was soaked repeatedly. I would have liked to get off that road, but there were no side streets that I could turn onto. As each car drove past, the headlights illuminated the drops of falling rain, which glimmered gold like particles of light. This registered as beautiful to me, but I could no longer bear the chill that I felt throughout my body, or the accompanying discomfort of being wet.

The road turned into a bridge that spanned a river, and on just this side of the bridge there was a gentle slope carpeted with grass, which I headed down. For now, I only wanted to get out of the rain. I figured I could stop under this huge bridge and smoke a cigarette while I thought about what to do next. Approaching the river, the ground went from grass to concrete, and both sides of the embankment were also faced with concrete. The river was high because of the rain, and it flowed swiftly and noisily. I ducked under the bridge, closing my umbrella. The sound of the river echoed under the bridge, making it seem remarkably louder. I found the noise extremely unpleasant. I wished I were back in my apartment, as I usually was, so I wouldn't have to listen to it. I was fed up with everything, but I knew that I had no one to blame but myself. I lit a cigarette, and looked for a place where I might be able to sit for the time being.

Right then, over by where the lawn turned to concrete, I thought I saw a dark silhouette, in the shape of a person. I considered that it might have just been some trash lying there, though the shadow looked a little too much like a man. I was immediately struck by a desire to flee. I felt a mixture of discomfort and unease, a complicated awareness that didn't take long to morph into fear. But my impulse to run away did not exceed my sense of curiosity. I focused my attention and approached cautiously. After taking two or three steps closer, I could tell for sure that it was a man. At that moment, I experienced a sharp jolt to my heart. He was wearing a black suit, lying facedown with his left arm stretched out limply above his head. I could feel my heart starting to race, fast and loud. I swallowed my saliva repeatedly in an attempt to moisten my throat, which had gone dry.

I came right up next to the man. He had short hair with a hint of gray, which made him appear to be in his fifties. His head was turned to the side, so I could see him quite clearly. I would have expected him to have a terrible look on his face, but there was something quite calm in his expression. His features had hardened, as if he were staring sullenly at something. Neither of his eyes was completely open, and his mouth was almost closed—there was nothing disgusting running out of it either. On the concrete where his head lay, there was a dark pool of liquid that, based on present circumstances, I assumed to be blood. For whatever reason, I couldn't stop staring at the blades of grass that stuck out from between the fingertips of the man's left hand. His suit jacket was flipped up in the back and I could see a little bit of his white shirt. I don't know why, but that white held my gaze for a long time too. The man's body retained a vigor, and exuded a sense of presence—the concrete and the lawn actually seemed like they were there for his sake. That didn't make any sense, though, because the man was dead. I stood there, as if rooted to the spot, but after a while the pounding of my heart gradually settled down, and finally I managed to regain my composure. This surprised me a little, the fact that I had started to get used to this scene, to this situation.

Not far from the man's right hand, I noticed the dark, clear-cut shadow of an object. I must have only become aware of it because I had started to accustom myself to the dead man. My heart started beating fiercely again, ringing in my ears. It felt like my heart was pounding even more wildly now than when I first saw him. I crouched down over the spot to get a better look at the dark object. I picked it up and brought it close to my face. I had no strength in my arm, so it took a lot of effort to maintain that position. I could feel an intense joy spreading throughout my body. And at the same time, to think that I felt such excitement at the mere sight of it—that I was filled with such delight—was disturbing. I had the sense of being torn in two. The elation seemed to escalate, independent of my own will, and I feared that I wouldn't be able to control myself. But I couldn't stop it, or pull myself back together. It wasn't long before the joy exceeded my tolerance level, and for a moment I was carried away. My heart throbbed painfully, my vision narrowed and, at the edge of my consciousness, I could tell that everything was growing blurry. It occurred to me—from this day on, the gun was mine. These words, which must have been generated by me, repeated themselves inside my head. The pleasure of that repetition, the bewildering pleasure—I had never experienced such a sense of fulfillment. Before long, my mind seemed to catch up with the joy, and I consciously repeated those words to myself. I even felt a slight blur of tears in my eyes. It was as if—I don't know—as if I forgave myself for feeling that way. Who knows, maybe I had already lost my mind. But now that I am able to make an even-tempered judgment, even if I was out of my head at the time, I think it was only temporary.

Soon after the joy flooded through me, I remembered that a person was lying dead only a short distance away. But I no longer cared about him. He was just some guy I didn't know, a stranger. I shoved the gun into the back pocket of my jeans, covering it with my shirt. I think I probably had a smile on my face. Now in high spirits, I had the urge to do something clever; I thought about calling up the police to tell them that I'd found a body.

But that seemed like it would be too much trouble. My next thought was that I ought to stay out of this, as much as possible. They might think that I was the one who killed this guy and, since above all my intention was to make off with the gun in hand, I might already be liable for a crime, legally speaking. I cautiously surveyed my surroundings, the same way that someone who had committed a murder would, and checked that there were no witnesses. Then I scrutinized the area for traces of myself, making sure that I hadn't dropped anything before I left. I projected a deliberately calm expression; I didn't hurry, I walked at a purposely slow pace. I paid particular attention when I emerged from the grassy slope back onto the street. I remained hidden in the shadow of the bridge, waiting patiently for a break in the stream of passing cars, so that I wouldn't be seen by anyone. I tried to concentrate on even the slightest sound, but it was hard to hear over the noise of the rushing cars and the raging river. Timing it just right as I emerged, I was careful to maintain a composed look on my face. I walked away slowly, going so far as to make it look as though I were pondering something, aware that someone might be watching. Then I realized that I was walking along without using my umbrella, so I hastily opened it. I was suffused with a joy that would not subside. The spray from the cars drenched me all over again, but I no longer minded in the least. My attention remained focused on the way the gun felt in my back pocket. At one point, unable to contain myself, I ducked into the shadow of a building to pull out the gun. The way it appeared in the light from the street was exceedingly beautiful. But now I realized that it was covered with crimson blood, smeared in particular around the end from which the bullets fired. I was stunned; it seemed strange to me that I hadn't noticed this when I first discovered the gun. I remembered that I had a packet of tissues shoved in my pocket and, moistening them with rainwater, I used them all up to wipe off the gun. I stuffed the now bloodstained tissues into the right front pocket of my jeans. I had no choice— there was nowhere to throw them away. It wasn't until after I finished wiping the gun off that it occurred to me that there was no need to have done such a thing right here and now. Once again, I surveyed my surroundings, checking that no one had seen me. There was no sound other than the rain drumming against the ground and the buildings—the neighborhood was so quiet it was unsettling. I exhaled a breath, savoring my sense of relief, and took one more look at the gun, confirming its magnificence. Then, as if to seal in that beauty, I hastily shoved it into the other back pocket of my jeans. I almost felt as if by exposing it for too long out in the open like that, its beauty might escape. I started walking slowly, in an effort to contain the heightened emotions coursing through my entire body. Maintaining that pace, this time I headed steadily back home.

I opened the door to my apartment, slowly went inside, and turned the lock. Standing in the middle of the wooden floor of my tiny apartment, I took out the gun I had just acquired. Looking at it, I could again feel joy spreading throughout my body. The gun was a little larger than the palm of my hand, the metal a rivetingly deep shade of silver-black. The tip of the barrel that the bullets were fired through was short, and the part next to that was molded to resemble the gills of a fish. In the center was a cylindrical contraption that must have held the bullets and, I figured, when this rotated it carried a bullet where it was supposed to go. Embedded right under this cylinder, there was a screw with the shape of a minus on its head, which signified to me that this was a man-made device. The part that I held in my hand was a densely uniform brown, and in the middle there was a round gold inlay with a decorative design. From there down, the handle was carved with an intricate diamond mesh pattern, and there was another screw with the same minus sign. The design on the round gold inlay was the image of a horse. Rearing up on its hind legs, the horse had something like a spear in its mouth, and another one caught between its front legs. Above it, the letters COLT were engraved, and there was a faint dull spot, like a dark patina, around the T. The same emblem appeared on the flat part of the silver-black metal as well—I had no idea what it meant, except that it had to symbolize something. On the left side of the barrel that the bullets fired from were engraved letters: LAWMAN MK III 357 MAGNUM CTG. I assumed this was the name of the gun, but it seemed more like a code. MAGNUM or MK III sounded awesome to me. And it felt good in my hand—it was uncanny how quickly I had gotten used to holding it. When I grasped it as if to take aim, without thinking each of my fingers found their proper position, comfortably steadying both the gun and myself. My thumb and index finger each moved purposefully to engage the hammer and the trigger, while the others supported them so naturally, taking on a shape as if my fingers had been meant to fit there. I knew I would never tire of the taut excitement transmitted through my skin where it made contact with the gun. The metal had such a deep luster, I stood and admired it in my grasp for a moment. I could have stayed like that forever, but it occurred to me that the gun was now mine, and I could look at it whenever I liked. I carefully examined it to see whether there were still any bloodstains, and when I found any I wiped them off right away, rubbing the whole thing over and over with a towel. Then I looked around my apartment, searching for a place where I could stash the gun.

In a corner of the room, I found a brown leather satchel and picked it up. It had been a present from a girl I had dated for only a month, a long time ago. I had been using it to store my insurance card, my official seal, the lease for this apartment, things like that. I dumped out all its contents and placed the gun inside. I felt like it was missing something, and after thinking for a minute, I spread a few white tissues underneath it. As I placed the gun back on top, I was filled with a sense of satisfaction. I stared at it for a moment, and then I practically had to force myself to close the flap and fasten the clasp.

• • •

THE EVENTS OF that night seem like a giddy dream to me. Even now, in my memory, they have a different quality, more pronounced, and for that reason, they lack a sense of reality. To me, reality always meant tedium. A few seconds after waking up, I recalled the events of the previous night, and again I was filled with that same joy. But then the joy turned to worry, and I hastily opened the leather bag. There was the gun, securely inside. Even if I doubted my reality, the mere fact of the gun there indicated its existence. I gazed upon the gun with fresh eyes. Once again, its overwhelming beauty and presence did not disappoint. I felt as though I might be transported—that is to say, that the world within myself could be unlocked—I felt full of such possibilities.

2

THREE DAYS HAD passed since I acquired the gun. There were no noticeable changes to my life—at least, superficially, there had been no shift. Everything around me was as tedious and boring as ever, but my spirits remained high. The change had occurred inside me.

I woke up each morning, as always, and the first thing I did was open the bag to make sure the gun was there. Then I got dressed quickly, put on my shoes, and went out. In the past, I often forgot to lock the door, but these three days, not once did that happen. This was hardly surprising, considering that I was leaving the gun behind in my apartment.

I looked up at the perfectly blue sky and thought about how the rain had finally stopped. For the past three days, the rain had continued to fall as if it some kind of spell had been cast. I was aware that I actually said to myself, *The rain has finally ended*, but that was because I was in a good mood, which was also why I peeked into my mailbox. I thought I might even allow myself to try the kinds of things normal people usually did.

I got on the subway and headed toward the university. The school's campus was crowded with students, and the riotous mix of colors from the clothes they were wearing hurt my eyes a little. A number of people I knew called out to me, and I smiled at each of them and said a few words in response. I entered a big dingy white building and went up the stairs. On my way, a guy bumped against my shoulder as he passed, and knocked me a little off balance. The guy muttered a simple apology and kept going. He was really rushing, like he must have been in some kind of hurry. At that moment, I had the idea to run after him, to chase him and try to knock him down. Doing so would surely take him by surprise, and shock whoever was watching. I was fascinated, imagining such a scene. Even just coming up with an idea like that must have been another sign that I was in a good mood.

Someone tapped me on the shoulder from behind, and I turned around to see Keisuke. He was smiling as usual. "How come you're just standing there?" he asked me. I was a little taken aback, and I laughed without answering his question. He looked at me and said, "Did something good happen to you?"

Keisuke kept talking. "The other day," he was saying, "I ended up just taking her home, like an idiot. I must have really been out of it. In the car, she was talking to me about all kinds of things, she was crying—think I felt like hitting on her? I just got outta there. I did the right thing, seriously, I did. I ended up cheering her up and all."

"Seriously? You really must have been out of it. You usually go in for the kill."

"Yeah, you know me, going for the kill. Like you should talk, Nishikawa," Keisuke said, laughing. He had started to walk alongside me. That's when I remembered that we had the next lecture together, that we always had.

Keisuke rattled on about girls, about his paper, about the CDs he'd bought recently.

After attendance had been taken and the lecture began, Keisuke gave a big yawn and promptly fell asleep next to me. Someone touched the back of my head, and I turned around to see a girl there. She said to me, "Haven't seen you in a while," but I didn't know who she was.

The bespectacled lecturer started talking in a low, subdued voice about globalization in the world, and about how American culture occupied a major position in it. As he passed out papers to the students, he spoke slowly about how America developed as a country while absorbing the cultures of various peoples. However, he went on to say, even a place as tolerant as America was still besieged by problems such as ethnocentrism and ghettoization.

"What is so powerful about American culture"—he got this far and then sneezed once, loudly—"however, is America's diversity itself. The Americanization of Japan is nothing new, but I would hate to think that it demonstrates a scarcity of Japanese culture. Yet the longing for American culture has existed since our defeat in the war up through the present day . . ."

As I was half-listening, I had also been replying to questions, one by one, from the girl sitting behind me. She said she was bored so she asked if I wanted to go to the cafeteria with her, but I didn't feel like it so I declined. At some point I realized that she was gone, although I had no idea when she had left.

In the middle of taking notes, I stopped and let my thoughts drift to the gun I had left behind in my apartment. I wondered why the gun held such boundless fascination for me, why I still felt such excitement about it being there. I led a boring life. It stood to reason that the gun would act as a stimulant within such tedium. I must have appreciated its absolute simplicity. The minimalism of the gun's shape epitomized the act of firing bullets even as it conveyed cruelty. I could think only of it causing injury, of destroying life; it had been created expressly so that a person could commit such deeds, its design utterly compact, nothing extraneous. It seemed to me a symbol, like Thanatos, the god of death himself. Yet it was difficult to determine why I was so mesmerized by such a lethal object. It wasn't as if I harbored the desire to kill someone. Nor did I yearn to kill myself. The thing is, up to then, I never expected to have anything to do with a gun. The idea occurred to me that I might be just like a child, thrilled by the acquisition of an unusual plaything, and that was what I liked best about it. There was no need to dwell on it. Whatever the case was, the gun was mine, and the pleasure I took from that had enabled me to pass each day since with relative ease. That, to me, was an important fact. To use the gun, to do something with it—the circumstances I now found myself in, that allowed for such a possibility, was the best part. I could use the gun to threaten someone, or I could use it to protect someone. I could kill someone, or I could even easily commit suicide. Rather than the question of whether or not I would actually do those things, or whether or not I wanted to, what was important was being in possession of that potential—that incarnation of stimulus itself.

When the lecture was almost over, Keisuke opened his eyes and said something to me. I wasn't really listening to him, so I just gave a vague answer. After class, Keisuke walked beside me as I left the classroom. He asked if I wanted to go to the cafeteria, and I realized that I was hungry. I decided to go along with him to get something to eat.

"You're coming to the speed dating thing tonight, right? I don't know how many people will be there, but I think the girls will be hot. It won't be any fun if you don't come along—you know I need my wingman, right?" Keisuke said, laughing jovially. I thought of the gun, and declined. But Keisuke wouldn't take no for an answer.

"Come on, I'm serious—I haven't had sex for a while now. It's been like a month. Really. I'm going to lose it if I don't get some. I need you on my team—you can have the hot one. It'll be worth your while."

"It makes no difference if I'm there or not."

"No, man, it matters to me. You always know how to come through for me. Like before, you got those two chicks to come out with us, didn't you? You could do it again."

Keisuke was so persistent, I had no choice but to give in. I regretted it as the image of the gun flickered in my mind. I had been thinking that today I would go out and buy some white cloth to lay under the gun. Then again, it might not be so bad to delay my gratification.

Keisuke and I killed some time, then headed to the bar. For some reason, the air conditioning was on inside, and I felt a little cold in the artificial chill. "We've been waiting for you," I heard someone say, and I saw Nakanishi. Keisuke and I had made a conscious decision to show up later than we were supposed to. It drew more attention, and somehow it was better to seem like you weren't really all that enthusiastic. Nakanishi was sitting at a large table with four girls and a guy whose face I recognized. I had only met him recently, and even though he had told me his name at the time, I couldn't quite remember it. Keisuke and I made up an excuse for being late, and Keisuke must have said something funny, because they all laughed at the same time. Two of the girls were awful, and the other two were average. Predictably, Keisuke and I chatted up the average-looking pair. We all left the bar and headed to a karaoke place. For whatever reason—maybe because they were drunk— both of the ugly girls were really hyped up, and they kept touching me. Every so often Nakanishi and I caught each other's eye and couldn't keep from smirking. One of the ugly girls was a good singer, and she seemed to know it, because she sang a lot of songs. She sputtered a lot, though, and since I was next to her, her saliva landed on me repeatedly.

I went to the toilet, and Keisuke showed up a little later. "I'm definitely gonna get some tonight," he said. "She's not all that cute, but that doesn't matter to me tonight." All I could do was laugh at him. I saw one of the average-looking girls heading toward the toilet, and I called out to her. "You look a little down," I said, and she told me she was stressed about her boyfriend, and she really hadn't planned on coming here tonight. I said that I wasn't really in a partying mood either, I felt more like having a quiet drink, and I mentioned the idea of going somewhere else. Keisuke said, "There's no reason to force it if you're not in the mood," glancing at me for some reason. Then we got her to send a text to the other average-looking girl to come over and join us, and the four of us left the bar together. Keisuke texted Nakanishi, hiding his smirk. I asked him what he'd written and Keisuke said that he'd asked Nakanishi to take care of the others. He smirked again. As I laughed with him, I noticed that the first girl looked really upset. I knew that most girls liked to talk about whatever was stressing them out. I stared at the pair of them, not really feeling up to it. Still, I focused on the one with bigger breasts as I thought about what to do next. Normally in this kind of situation, I would play the nice guy and go home, but because of the gun, I had been in such a good mood these last few days. I made up my mind to do it tonight, just like Keisuke.

He and I chose a quiet bar, and we listened to the girls talk. We ordered strong drinks for them, and sympathized with whatever they said, caring expressions on our faces. At one point, the girls started to feel guilty about sneaking out of the karaoke bar, but Keisuke and I told them not to worry about it. "Just tell them we forced you to leave, or we were begging and crying, so you were freaked out and followed us. Make us the bad guys, so they won't blame you or the other girls. I mean, we were the ones who asked you to go anyway, weren't we," Keisuke said, laughing a bit, though I wasn't sure why.

After a little time had passed, I thought I'd give it a shot, so I touched the hand of the girl who I had been talking to the most, then caressed her hair, and she made no move to resist. *Seems like the time is right*, I thought to myself, and I decided to stop drinking. Then I left the bar with the girl.

We took a taxi to the building where the girl lived, and I went into her apartment. She seemed pretty drunk, but I suspected that she wasn't really as tipsy as she was pretending to be. I threw her down on the bed and undressed her. I decided to pay special attention to her body. Normally, at this point, I basically did whatever I felt like. Plenty of times, I just came whenever I was ready to. But, this time, I proceeded cautiously and deliberately, watching for her response to whatever I did. I chalked it up to my recently improved mood. She moaned a lot, and I focused on that while I took as much time as I was capable of.

3

I WOKE UP in the girl's apartment. I had intended to leave before she woke up, but I must have been tired, because the girl was no longer beside me in bed. I heard a clink, followed immediately by the rushing sound of a flame. There was an earth-toned curtain that acted as a divider so I couldn't see, but I figured she must have been cooking something. The scent of her on the fingertips of my right hand made me nauseous. I reached out and grabbed my cigarettes from on top of the table, lit one, and inhaled. My discarded clothes were folded neatly at the foot of the bed in a way that made them seem like they weren't mine.

"Oh, I must have woken you up. Sorry," she said, peeking through the curtain. It being morning, she was made up simply, and she was wearing a white sweatshirt. I liked what she said to me, it made me feel satisfied. The words she had spoken were common and ordinary, yet there was something indescribably good about them. Searching for an appropriate response, I said, "No, that's okay." I thought that sounded inadequate, so I added, "What time is it?"

"It's already ten. Too late to make second period. I didn't really feel like going anyway."

"Nine? I guess I thought it was earlier."

"What? It's ten—not nine. I said ten," she said with a little laugh, then announced that she was making coffee.

I thanked her, and asked her to make it strong. I got up from the bed, and put on the folded clothes. Then I thought about what I should do now. I realized I could do anything in this situation. The old me had enjoyed these kinds of thrills, but it was hard for the new me to experience it the same way. They say that a person can get used to anything, and I agree that is often true.

Call it self-centered, but I felt nothing more than weary annoyance about what to do next.

I put out my cigarette, and walked into the kitchen where she was making coffee. She had her back to me, and I wrapped my arms around her body from behind. Aware that I was being vulgar, I touched her breasts and ran my mouth along the nape of her neck. I did it so that she would think I was the worst kind of guy, only interested in her body, and the idea that maybe I was that guy made me smirk. She laughed, too, and pressed against my chest as she said, "Wait a minute." I put my right arm between her legs, roughly sliding my hand over her sex through the denim of her jeans. I said, "Lemme do it one more time. I only got a taste last night, I need some more." I waited for her to get angry at me. I thought she might throw the boiling water on the burner at me, which I supposed would have been a reasonable thing to do. I resigned myself to whatever was going to happen next. I took great pleasure in the act of choosing to surrender myself. But she burst into laughter.

"Okay, I get it, but you don't need to be all over me—I mean, if you really want to do it, that's fine. Just wait for the coffee. I have a boyfriend, but we can see each other when you like, if that's all right with you," she said, not taking me seriously.

I didn't know how to react, but what she was suggesting didn't sound all that bad to me. I decided that I would go home after I had some coffee.

I chain-smoked cigarettes while channel surfing on her television. I finally settled on NHK. Numerous people were climbing a snowy mountain in winter. A man whose face was snow-burned a deep brown said something to the men and women surrounding him, and everyone laughed out loud.

The girl placed the coffee and plates of toast on the table. The aroma of the coffee wafted through the room, and as I took a sip, the pleasing bitterness slid down my throat. I complimented her on the coffee, and she told me that she worked in a coffee house. "I get ground beans from there. You should stop by some time, it tastes much better in the café," she said, taking a sip.

The program ended and the news came on the television screen. A man wearing a suit described the situation in Afghanistan, and the broadcast showed a hospital somewhere. A man missing a leg was lying on a dingy bed, and when he realized he was on camera, he scowled. The camera drew closer, focusing on his contorted face. He spoke in his cryptic language. *I'm a mule trader*. The Japanese subtitles flashed across the bottom of the screen. *But all my mules were burned with my house, and I lost my leg. I know nothing about politics, and I don't care.* He appeared to still be talking, but the scene shifted to a desert landscape.

The girl talked about various things, and I made responsive sounds at the appropriate moments. I nibbled on the toast and drank the coffee. The bread was still warm, and I realized how long it had been since I'd eaten toast. I looked around her apartment, which was decorated uniformly with furniture in mellow shades of brown, and the walls were such a fresh white it almost hurt my eyes. There was a large stuffed bear on top of the bookcase, and when I stared at it she smiled and told me that her boyfriend had bought it for her.

The screen changed again, and I saw the words, MAN'S BODY FOUND AT ARAKAWA RIVER. I grasped the coffee cup with my fingers, my attention absorbed by the report. I experienced a sharp jolt to my heart; it felt as though I had been injected with something and couldn't move. "Yesterday, the twenty-fourth," the man on the television said, "the body of a man was discovered near the Arakawa River in Tokyo's Itabashi Ward. The man had been shot in the head, and it appears that approximately five days had passed since the time of death. The man appeared to be in his forties or fifties; his identity has not been made public. The Tokyo Metropolitan Police Department is treating this as a homicide, and has begun a criminal investigation, including inquiries regarding the whereabouts of the possible murder weapon."

The news then switched over to sports—Ichiro had a hit and the Mariners had won. A Westerner whom I didn't recognize was holding a press conference and speaking proudly about something. Some guy on a golf course was holding a silver cup; horses were running. I had fallen silent, and the girl turned to say something to me. I responded to her, trying to maintain my composure.

"What's the matter? You look white as a sheet."

"What?"

"Your face—you've gone pale as a ghost."

I couldn't comprehend what she was saying. Thinking she must be making fun of me, I laughed. I meant to laugh out loud, but my voice was hoarse, and all that escaped from my throat was a strained sigh. My vision became dim, and some time passed before I realized that I had been staring at her for quite a while. At the edge of my consciousness, the word "bathroom" flickered, and I managed to tell the girl that I was going to the bathroom. She said something to me about being worried. I went into the bathroom and looked in the mirror. My face was ashen, as if white paint had oozed from every pore of my skin. There was sweat on my brow, and a chill went up and down my spine. I felt a tingle along the inside of both arms, like I had virtually no strength. I splashed water on my face, and then for some reason, drank some. I thought the contact with water would bring back some feeling to my face. There was a knock on the door, and it gave me quite a start. "Are you okay?" I heard a voice that must have been her. I muttered to myself, *What the hell are you doing? Everything is going to be fine.*

Through the door I said, "Uh, sorry, I, uh, kind of threw up. I'm really sorry. Yeah, I'll be fine."

"What? Oh, I was afraid of that. But the bread was still fresh—oh, no, I'm so sorry."

"No, that's not it—sometimes, this happens for no reason. I guess it's just how I am."

"Oh, I'm sorry, really—should I call an ambulance, or something?"

"No, no. I'm fine. It's nothing, really. I'm better now. I always feel better right after."

Staring in the mirror, I could feel laughter starting to well up. I was getting ahead of myself, I thought. After all, I didn't kill that guy. For all I knew, he might have committed suicide. But then it occurred to me. Since I had made off with the gun from the scene, his death was considered a murder. If the weapon that caused his death were not at the scene, it was unlikely to be deemed a suicide, which must be why the police were treating it as a homicide. And, at least as far as the police were concerned, whoever had the gun was the criminal. I was still a little worked up, but I managed to pull myself back together. I had figured all along this would happen, ever since that night. None of this was outside of my expectations. At the time, I had been very careful when I left the scene of the crime— nothing there could be traced to me, and there were no witnesses. There was no way for anyone to know that I was in possession of the gun. I was safe, I thought to myself. And as long as I didn't make any mistakes, the gun would remain mine.

Nevertheless, I was a little surprised that I hadn't been checking regularly for this in the news. I ought to have been actively seeking information about when they would discover the man's body, and how the police were conducting their investigation from the outset. The fact that I hadn't done so was probably because I had been on such a high. It must have taken them so long to find him because of the days of rain. Under normal circumstances, nobody ever went near that darkened bridge, much less when it was raining. It seemed like I should be grateful that it had taken so long to discover him. I felt like I had been saved, despite my lack of attention. At least now, the police and I were on the same starting line, and I would be fine as long as I went about it carefully. There was no reason for anyone to associate me with the dead guy. At the thought that sooner or later the case would be forgotten, I felt a sensation of relief mixed with joy, as the strength once again seeped out of my body. I thought to myself, it was possible that this tension, and even my sense of relief at having overcome this looming crisis, could transform into a kind of enjoyment.

I then had sex with the girl one more time. I got the impression that she wasn't all that into it, but I was feeling good and was up for it. I think I might have really worn her out. After I came, I stroked her hair. I did that for a while, despite the fact that she was certainly not a beauty. Then I made a joke to get her to laugh, and added, "I'll be back sometime."

4

I WENT TO the department store in my neighbor-hood, where I bought two white handkerchiefs. I finally had the chance to get something to lay under the gun inside the bag. The handkerchiefs were made of cupro fabric—smooth to the touch, like silk—exactly like what I had imagined. I thought the gun's colors, the riveting silver-black as well as the vibrant brown, reminiscent of natural wood, would stand out beautifully atop this velvety white. I also bought another handkerchief made of the same fabric but in black. I thought I would use that one to polish the gun. My gun was so beautiful, I didn't think it needed to be polished, but I liked the idea of polishing it and wanted to anyway. Through the act of polishing it, I thought I might be able to communicate more deeply with the gun.

I was eager to get back to my apartment, so I quickened my pace. No matter how much I walked, I didn't feel tired. I went over the railway crossing and cut across a park, breaking into a run midway. My cell phone rang, and I was a little surprised by how loud it sounded. Reflexively, I answered; it was my mother calling. She asked me if anything new had happened. When I said, "Why do you ask?" she told me that she had had a dream about me.

"It's just that, you know, seeing you in my dream all of a sudden, I was worried that something might have happened."

"Come on, you freak me out with that kind of thing."

"No, for some reason I was just worried—so you haven't caught a cold? Are you all right?"

"I'm fine. Look, I'm kind of busy right now, sorry, I have to go," I said and hung up, even though it seemed like my mother still had something else she wanted to say.

She always called my apartment whenever she needed to speak to me. I wondered for a moment why she had decided to call my cell phone, but then my thoughts turned once again to the gun. There were two things for me to do today. I had just completed the first—buying the white cloths—and the second was to examine the bullets inside the gun. Whether bullets were loaded securely inside was, as far as I was concerned, a critical issue. So critical, in fact, that, terrified of confirming whether or not they were there, I had not dared investigate before today. This was a habit of mine, putting off matters of grave importance. It was less about not wanting to kill my joy; rather, I preferred to cling to grand illusions. However, I could not just avoid this forever. If there were no bullets inside, my gun would lose some of its significance. I mean, even if I never actually used the gun, it needed to have bullets in it. If it weren't loaded, then one way or another I would need to get my hands on some bullets. And doing so would be fraught with considerable peril and challenges. It was a choice I hoped to avoid, if possible.

What concerned me was the high probability that the man lying there had in fact killed himself. How many bullets would he load in the gun he would use to commit suicide? He could have loaded a single bullet and then taken his own life. I guessed that would have been the usual way to do it. This was a nagging suspicion in my mind. When I became aware of this doubt I harbored, I grew anxious, sometimes to the point where I couldn't stand it. I realized I could no longer put it off. I needed to know for certain what my situation was.

I returned to my apartment and opened the satchel. The gun was as breathtakingly beautiful as ever. The girl I had just slept with was no comparison for the gun. In this moment, the gun was everything to me, and would be everything to me from now on as well. As I pondered whether or not it was loaded, I gazed at its piercing metallic sheen.

I made up my mind that I would try to pull the cylindrical piece in the center out sideways. In my imagination, bullets could be loaded one by one, by moving this part out to either the left or right. Figuring that was a safe bet, I proceeded, careful not to touch the trigger or the hammer. My hands trembled slightly with nervousness, and I felt my body dampening with a cold sweat. As I pushed it with the ball of my thumb, the cylinder made a little clink and moved far out to the left, stopping at a point where I could see clearly inside. There were four golden bullets loaded in it. Each of the gold bullets was embedded in one of the six regularly spaced holes. For a moment, I gave myself over to a sense of bewildering joy that was mingled with excitement and relief. This was as it should be, I thought. The gun would never betray me, it would satisfy me in every way, I said to myself as I could feel a smile breaking out across my face. I stared at the bullets and imagined them being fired from the gun and how far they would travel. I couldn't call to mind a more beautiful image, or something so fascinating. Then, without hesitation, I visualized myself using the gun. First I leveled the gun, and with my right thumb I lowered the hammer. Then I closed my left eye, focusing my right eye as I decided on an appropriate target. What *should* I shoot? I hadn't thought about it. For instance, I wondered, a person? Anyone would do— some hopeless lowlife who deserved to be shot—that's who I'd aim for. I imagined a woman. A man would also do, but the first thing that popped into my mind was an unknown woman, slender with long hair. Preparing for the impact, I braced my right wrist, grasping it with my left hand. I placed my right index finger on the trigger, and slowly pulled it toward me. The impact of the gunshot rippled through my entire body, a dense and fine vibration running along my wrist. Of course I couldn't see the actual bullet fly out, but I thought I saw a spark of discharge and a plume of smoke that accompanied it. The bullet bore through the woman's body, and as she fell blood spurted out. She might say something as she lay there. But that's where I took leave of my fantasy. I had no penchant for so-called subversive impulses or brutality. For example, I was capable of unflinchingly watching a movie in which a monster eats someone's guts out, but it didn't excite me in any way. I had no particular desire to see a woman writhing in agony. My interest was simply in the kind of excitement derived from the act of destroying some form of life, and in the extraordinariness of that. It was the process, rather than the outcome; more than the blood and gore on the screen, it was the tension evoked by what I saw that aroused my interest.

I lay down on my bed and wondered about who first thought up such a device and decided to create it. I imagined the gun's predecessor must be something like a cannon, which developed into a long rifle, like a musket, before evolving into a pistol. Naturally, it goes without saying, they all shared the common purpose of killing living things. A knife or a sword served the same objective, but what was fundamentally different about these was the risk involved. In order to kill someone with a knife, you needed to get close to him. The implication being that you would likely be prone to a counterattack—that is to say, someone trying to kill you—this was the specific risk involved. But that wasn't the case with a gun. Of course, if the other guy had a gun too then it would turn into a shootout, but you could take aim from a protected position, and if you hit your target, your foe might die without knowing who killed him. On the part of the killer, it still guaranteed a considerable—not to say absolute—degree of safety, compared to a knife or a sword. As well as the fact that there would be virtually no immediate sensation of having killed someone—no slicing through flesh or shattering bones. Naturally the killer must experience something, but with a gun, it was only the impact of the bullets being fired; there was no point of contact with your foe's flesh and bone. It didn't require the effort of a cannon or a bow and arrow, nor did it expose your own person to the danger of a bomb or the like. A pistol was even more portable than a rifle, all it took was the pull of your fingertip. The silver of the metal seemed to embody the desire of the inventor who sought an easy way to kill someone. It made me a little uncomfortable to put words like "ease" and "death" together. Once again, I picked up this device that equated such contradictory concepts in my hand, and I studied it closely. The gun brought murder closer, and yet, it seemed to enable the murderer himself to stand by and watch the crime being committed. And it came in such a beautiful shape. I thought that its creator must have made it look this way in order to arouse the desire to acquire it, or perhaps it was through this proximity to death that its shape evolved organically, and that was what the creator found beautiful. Yet an arrow or a knife were also beautiful in the same way. Did people experience beauty in things that were associated with death? Or is that what they sought? I turned these thoughts over, but I couldn't be sure. I decided that I wasn't supposed to understand.

I lit a cigarette, and I lay the two white handkerchiefs I had bought in the bag before placing the gun on top of them. I added the black cloth as well, and took another look. Now that I knew there were bullets inside, the gun seemed to possess an even stronger presence, even more persuasiveness. My breath caught, as I stared at the gleaming silver-black and the deep brown. At that moment, what I felt toward its riveting presence was a sense of awe. Its presence seemed far greater than that of myself. I wondered if I could actually possess something such as this. With its distinct purpose, and its diverse potential, would it allow me to be its owner? I thought about this as I pulled on my cigarette relentlessly, and when it was finished, I closed the flap of the bag.

I opened the refrigerator, then slowly drank a mineral water I took from inside. I was hungry, so I went to a nearby coffee shop, where I ordered coffee and a tuna sandwich with lettuce. The waitress was plump, and she was heavily made up. Bored by my surroundings, I slugged down the terrible coffee. A guy who seemed to be the owner was absentmindedly watching a small television that was set on the counter. Neither the waitress nor the owner seemed very enthusiastic about running the coffee shop. The television showed a montage of New York streetscapes. I figured that, in America, there were average citizens who owned a gun like the one I now had. For them, guns were just a part of everyday life, nothing particularly unusual about them. Yet the strange thing was that I did not envy them. I rarely yearned for anything out of the ordinary. It didn't much matter to me if everyone else had the same things as I did. The thing was that I had found it. The same way that, for instance, some people found pleasure drawing pictures or making music, or they relied on work or women, drugs or religion, I felt like I had discovered what I was passionate about. And for me, that thing was nothing more than the gun. There was nothing wrong with me. That's what I realized. And I started to relax—I lit a cigarette and leaned back in my chair.

5

I WENT TO the university, and attended a number of my lectures. Lately I had been getting to class often, and the reason was probably because I had the gun. Since I had found it, I had become more active, doing things that I normally found tedious. I handed in papers before they were due, I lent my notes to other students.

I headed over to the cafeteria, where I smoked cigarettes while drinking coffee. Keisuke drank coffee with me, and talked about girls. "This last one, she

was really something," he said, laughing in amusement. "She seemed pretty normal, but she could really
scream. I'm sure the people next door must have been
able to hear her." I doubted that Keisuke would stop
talking anytime soon. I just laughed at his stories, and
kept smoking.

"What about you? You got some, right? Tell me, how
was it?"

"Yeah, I got some. I think she'll even let me do it again
sometime."

"Huh? You mean you might be able to, like, date her?"

"No, just sex. She's got a boyfriend, so it's perfect,"
I said, and Keisuke laughed and said, "Nishikawa, you
really are a prick." It made no sense to me, but I laughed
anyway. Maybe Keisuke laughed too hard, because he
choked a little as he took a drag of his cigarette. For
some reason, I felt like being alone.

"But isn't that kind of risky? I mean, seriously, if her
boyfriend finds out, you'll get dragged into it. She'll
probably say she wants to dump him for you."

"I'll deal with that when it happens. Anyway, I don't
really care. I'll see her if I feel like it."

Keisuke laughed, and then he started telling me
about picking up girls on the street. I didn't have much

interest, but I nodded anyway, and kept on like that until he had to leave for his job.

Now that I was by myself, I ordered another coffee and drank it slowly. The voices of the students around me were annoying, and I thought about going some-where quieter. There was a guy at the table next to me, scribbling away furiously, seemingly oblivious to the noise surrounding him. I had the urge to interrupt him, but since I didn't know him, I restrained myself. A number of people I knew walked in; they called out to me, and I greeted each of them. It was a while until my next lecture, so I didn't know what to do. It occurred to me then that I probably should have brought the gun with me.

Someone tapped me, and I turned around to see a girl there. I didn't recognize her so I was quite sur-prised. She asked me what I was doing, and I replied that I was killing time. As I studied her face, gradually I realized that something about her seemed familiar, but that was only after talking with her for a while. I thought I remembered her talking to me from the row behind me during class before, and that she had said, "It's been a while." But I couldn't recall anything else about her. I had no choice but to act as though

I knew who she was, and watch as she took a seat at my table.

"University is so boring, isn't it? Lately I've been thinking of quitting again. But then, I've got two years to go."

"Well, there's no reason to quit, is there? Then again, what do I know?"

"Hmm, it's a tough call, I guess . . . I wish it was more interesting."

She wore a short black skirt with a fitted white sweater; she had large breasts and refined features. I searched through my memory as I stared at her, but I still couldn't recall who she was. Her dyed brown hair was very well-kempt, and it gleamed as it reflected the fluorescent light of the cafeteria. She looked directly at me, blinking her big eyes repeatedly, while she talked about this and that. Apparently she was frustrated about something, but I wasn't sure what it was. As I smoked my cigarette and observed her various mannerisms, I was aware of my sexual desire for her.

At moments like this, I often daydreamed about doing it with the girl. And then occasionally, when I acted on my own inclination, since that's what I always did, there were times when it ended up happening. It was more about following my own habit or pattern than about my own intention, but now, for some reason, I felt reluctant about asking her out somewhere, as I typically would have done. I had just slept with that other girl, and the thought of going through all those motions again seemed tedious to me. I figured this reluctance also had something to do with the gun, but I couldn't really tell whether that was the case because I had in fact slept with a girl since getting it. As she and I talked, I hesitated about what to do next. Ultimately, though, I reached the decision that I should ask her out. Whenever I got tired of wondering about something, I always went with the option that might yield a surprise.

"So, you really don't remember, do you?"

"Remember what?"

"I mean, really, you don't remember me, do you? You're forcing yourself. This whole time, you've had this full-of-shit look on your face," she said, studying me.

I stared at her, a little taken aback. A faint smile played about her lips as she watched my eyes. I had no choice but to admit she was right. I realized it might be possible that I had slept with this girl, but that was unlikely. In the first place, I didn't sleep with girls whose faces I'd forget, and I had never been so drunk that I'd blacked out. I apologized to her, and she laughed out loud.

"It's no big deal if you say you don't remember me. Really, it happens. It was ages ago anyway, now that I think about it. Like, when we were freshmen, there was a party for some club. It was a welcome party for incoming students or something. We left together and got something to eat, didn't we? I'm Yuko, Yuko Yoshikawa. Do you remember now?" she said, looking at me with a smile.

Hearing her describe it, I had a faint recollection of that time. I had definitely snuck out of that party with a girl named Yuko, and we had gotten dinner at some chain restaurant. And then something else had suddenly come up that I had to do, and I had forgotten all about her. But, as I recalled, that girl had had short black hair, and she seemed like a different person from the one here now. Obviously I didn't really remember, but there was something about Yuko's air that gave a much different impression from how she had been back then.

"A lot has happened since then. I was in America for a while. I took a leave of absence from school. I was doing something like a homestay, but I recently came back to school. Which I majorly regret now, really. I was bored over there too, but it's probably worse here. I guess it's the same, after all, wherever you go," she said, smiling again.

For whatever reason, I decided against asking her out. It might have been because I felt like she had called me a liar—I wasn't sure. But in any case, it was annoying to go through the same thing all over again in such a short time—it was exhausting, really. She ordered a coffee, apparently intending to sit and chat with me for a while. Her big eyes were her defining characteristic, and I couldn't stop staring at them. I lit yet another cigarette, and drank my already cold coffee.

"But, you know, you seem very different, really. Wasn't your hair short back then? I remember now. No, seriously. That must have been amazing, going to America. I mean, my English is terrible."

"English? Oh, well, it's really no big deal to be able to speak it. Basically now I can have a conversation with an English-speaker, you know? It's not as if I started studying it because I liked it. That was all my parents. They forced me to take English classes when I was little."

"Hmm, but didn't that work out for you in the end though?"

"Well, I guess, but I don't really know. One day they'll probably make an automatic translator or something, and then there won't be any need for it. Right? I'm sure that will happen. So, enough about that, what have you been doing? Did you repeat a year or something?"

"Nope. I've just been going to class, same as usual."

"Hmm, really? Sounds pretty boring."

Then she said she felt like doing something fun. I wasn't quite sure what she meant, so I asked her specifically what she wanted to do. She said that she didn't really know herself, so she would leave it up to me. She added that she remembered that she had fun the first time we hung out. I figured she'd be awfully surprised if I were to suggest that we have sex. I had a habit of wanting to turn what seemed like was about to happen into something unexpected—a slight yet distinct fascination that I occasionally indulged. I hesitated for a moment, then decided to forget about it for now. She continued to make vague requests of me, which seemed to amuse her in some way. The fact was, I felt like she was trying to drag me down into her own boredom. I gave it some thought but I didn't come up with any good ideas. And I figured that, when bored people got together, they would only beget boredom. Something about that line appealed to me, and I wanted to try to remember it. The image of the gun flitted through my mind but it wasn't as if I was going to share that with her. Yuko and I continued to just hang out like that for quite a while.

She asked for my cell phone number, so I asked for hers too. Just then, an idea occurred to me, a sort of game. I would take my time, and in due course, become close friends with this Yuko Yoshikawa. I liked the idea of it taking a long time. Rather than trying to have sex with her right away, I would try, little by little, to proceed along the course. It may have sounded ridiculous, but something about it appealed to me. If at some point, a boyfriend of hers were to appear on the scene, I might even try to act jealous. I felt my mood gradually begin to improve, and I was happy about that. And, for some reason, I still attributed the root of this shift for the better to the gun.

Outside the light was slowly fading, and little by little the air around us grew faintly blue. On campus, the outdoor lights came on, glowing orange, and crowds of students came and went among them, in conversation as they walked. The orange orbs glimmered as they cut through the dim blueness, and I may have stared at them too long, because an afterimage lingered in my vision. The imprint went from yellow to green, following my gaze wherever I looked. Trying to focus on the afterimage itself, the background appeared blue, then orange. As I did so, I experienced a slow, dreamy sensation. The feeling steadily enveloped me, and the next thing I knew, the moment slipped away. I had fallen asleep right then and there.

Yuko Yoshikawa was talking about something, and smoking one of my cigarettes. I nodded at what she said, and drank my coffee.

6

I POLISHED THE gun inside my apartment.

Of course I used the black cupro cloth that I bought previously, holding the gun in my left hand and the cloth in my right hand. While I moved around the apartment, I always carried the gun and the cloth with me, polishing it as I listened to music or watched television. I polished it with both elbows propped on the table, or while I was lying in bed.

Time went by surprisingly quickly this way. I took

pleasure in the monotony of the task, repeating a conversation with the gun. Needless to say, I didn't actually speak aloud to the gun, or even carry on a conversation in my head. The gun was a device, so talking to it was the same as talking to myself, and if the gun were to reply, that would mean I was crazy. I simply polished the gun in silence, constantly aware that I was near to the gun. As I did so, however, at times I felt an inexplicable twinge of sadness. I don't really know why, but it had been a very long time since I had felt that way. I wondered what the cause might be, but I couldn't figure it out. The day turned to evening, and eventually night.

These past few days, I had often seen the police in the neighborhood. I realized I might have noticed them more because I was hyper-alert to their presence, but it really did seem as though there were more of them around. I overheard a group of women near the convenience store saying that they had seen a lot of cops, and I eavesdropped on some male students speculating about the Arakawa murderer. One time I even saw a uniformed policeman accompanied by a dog, near a nature park about a kilometer from my building. That really shook me up. I had heard about sniffer dogs that could detect the scent of drugs, but I didn't know whether they were used for guns as well. It was unlikely, but there was no way to know for sure. The gun was metal, and other than that, I didn't think it gave off a particular scent. When I saw them, I watched the dog for a while, but it paid no attention to me, keeping its snout to the ground and sniffing at something intently.

I put the gun and the black cloth away in the satchel, and went out to buy something for dinner. There was a chill in the air, and having worn nothing over my shirt, I was cold. I lit a cigarette, and set out at a leisurely pace anyway. The sky was overcast with enormous clouds that obscured the moon and the stars.

I got as far as the convenience store, and then just kept going. I could have easily shopped there, but I felt like walking on further. Along the way, I bought a can of coffee from a vending machine and sipped it. I had wandered onto a narrow street lined with residences that I continued to follow, cutting through a bicycle parking lot and going over a railroad crossing. I passed several people, and almost collided with someone whizzing by on a bicycle. The rider was a young guy, and I sort of wished I had kicked his front tire. I walked pretty far and wore myself out, so I found a narrow concrete step built into the wall of a building and sat down. I berated myself a bit, wondering why I had kept walking to the point of exhaustion.

Just then, I saw a uniformed policeman riding toward me on a bicycle. He appeared to be on a neighborhood patrol, his gaze following his surroundings as he decelerated. Once he noticed me, our eyes met and held as he slowly approached. I was a little startled, but I reminded myself that this didn't mean anything, and I tried to manage an attitude of nonchalance. I was sitting by myself, on an empty back street, past ten o'clock at night. In such a situation, there was no reason a cop wouldn't question me. Conscious of trying to convince myself to be relieved, I braced for the officer. Thinking that it would seem even more suspicious to act as though I didn't see him, I stared back at him with a bland expression, trying to project a look that casually implied that it was unusual to see a policeman around here.

"Is anything the matter here?" he began by saying. I realized he was actually questioning me, and I felt slightly annoyed. He was young, probably almost the same age as I was, I figured. I had expected him to have a look of righteous and fearless determination, but he wore glasses that made his eyes seem round, and his cheeks were a little puffy. I took a drag off the cigarette in my hand, and exhaled the smoke into the air. Then I decided to act like someone who had been drinking.

"No, I'm a little drunk, so I'm just taking a break here. I'm about to be on my way."

"Ah, I see, but, it's not safe around here, so you should hurry up and get home."

"Not safe? Did something happen?"

"Lately there's been a high incidence of purse snatchings. Targeting young women, though."

"Purse snatchings? Oh, now that you mention it, I've seen a lot of flyers on billboards."

"That's right. Well, even men should be careful, it could happen at any time, so please be on your way."

"Yes, I understand. Thank you for your trouble."

"Not at all. Now, if you'll excuse me."

He gave a slight bow in my direction and then started to pedal off again somewhere on his bicycle. He seemed uninterested in me. I felt a little buzz, perhaps from talking to the cop. It may have come from the nervous tension I felt about the gun in my apartment and my relief that the conversation was over. Giving myself over to the excitement, I called after the policeman. He braked, turning only his head to say, "What is it?" My mood was extremely high—I was aware of a desire, for some reason, to curry favor with this guy. I realized I was getting carried away, but I felt no need to restrain myself.

"Um, were drugs found around here, by any chance?"

"What?"

"I mean, were there drugs, or something, found around here?"

Hearing my question, the cop's expression shifted, and he dismounted from his bicycle and approached me again. I noticed that his demeanor seemed slightly different. I was a little nervous, but at the same time, I was curious to see what would happen next.

"Excuse me, but why would you ask such a thing?"

"No, lately, I've seen policemen with dogs around. Are they called sniffer dogs? So, I just figured that's what it was. That something like that might have happened."

"Yes, but I'm not able to provide more details about the investigation. I'm sorry. The truth is, I don't know the details myself. However, a few days ago, in fact, the Tokyo Police arrested someone involved with a drug-related gang. Excuse me but, uh, why do you ask . . . ?" he said, as he started to study my face.

I wondered what the cop would do if I were to panic right now, but of course I didn't do that. I calmly smoked my cigarette, and gave a little smile. It made me aware of the nervous tension I was holding inside.

"I'm working on alternate theories for my thesis. I'm studying data on preventive measures for drugs and suicide, which is why I was wondering."

"Your thesis? For university?"

"That's right. My professor doesn't rely on books alone, he tells us we should go to the police and juvenile detention centers. So I just thought I would ask you. I'm sorry. I guess I do tend to get chatty when I drink."

He seemed unimpressed by what I said, but he also seemed to register relief. He gave a brief sigh and said, "I'd like to be of assistance but I have work to do myself." Then he told me again, "You should go home as soon as possible." I thanked him, and walked in the opposite direction of the cop. I thought that he too might have enjoyed that a little.

While I was walking, I thought about how much more nervous I would have been had I been carrying the gun with me. I probably would have been so anxious and scared, I wouldn't have been able to bear it. Needless to say, I didn't enjoy fear and anxiety for their own sake, but it piqued my interest, as it were, when they were mixed in with excitement. Maybe I should start walking around with the gun when I felt like it. Maybe that would lead to further discoveries.

Finally, I went into a convenience store and bought a bento and a juice, and headed back to my building. My legs were tired, and my heels ached. As I approached my door, I was a little surprised to see light coming through the small window of the kitchen of the apartment next door. It had been vacant until a few days earlier, when a moving company had brought in someone's belongings, but I had been unaware of signs that anyone was living there. I had thought that they must have rented it as a sort of storeroom or something, but tonight I realized that someone had moved in. Mine was the innermost apartment on the ground floor; sometimes I heard sounds from above, but until now it had been relatively quiet. I had a bad feeling, but reminded myself there wasn't anything I could do. I unlocked my front door and went into the apartment. I could hear noise, a child's voice mixed in with what must have been the sound of the television. Feeling bummed out, I turned up the volume on a Stones album to drown out the sounds. Then I thought about Yuko Yoshikawa, and wondered when I should call her.

7

AFTER MY LECTURE ended, I searched for Yuko Yoshikawa. Thinking I would run into her accidentally-on-purpose, I went to the cafeteria, and checked out each of several smoking areas on the quad. It didn't really matter to me whether or not I saw her, but I searched valiantly. Since she was a literature major, I even walked through her department's building, but was still unable to find her. I was just about to give up when it occurred to me to try calling her cell phone. I knew that I didn't need to go to such ends, but once I commit to doing something, I like to follow it through faithfully, so I thought I'd see if she wanted to have lunch. As I listened to the ringing tone, I noted how high my motivation level was today. And whatever the reason for it, being motivated wasn't such a bad thing.

I let the phone ring seven times, and then I hung up. I figured she might be with another guy or something right now. I just had a feeling, even though I had no idea if she was seeing anyone in particular. If she were dating a guy who played it cool, I would need to be a good listener, but if, on the other hand, he were the jealous, needy type, then I would have to be the cool one. In either case, blowing up her cell phone was not the thing to do, so I had to give it up for today. And— who knows—she might very well just call me up herself.

The gun was inside my bag. I had placed it in a black leather pouch, the opening of which was tied up securely, and put the pouch in my university bag. The pouch was American and expensive; it was well-made and completely concealed the gun, and most importantly, I liked its plain and simple design. Since I had started carrying the gun around with me, I had been going about my life very conscientiously. If I were to leave the bag somewhere, or if I were mugged, that would be the end of me. Now, every day was filled with a pleasant tension, and I felt a constant, piercing excitement that welled up from deep inside my body. The knowledge that I was carrying a gun made me hyperaware of almost everything else in my life. In the middle of a lecture, I often pulled the leather pouch out of my bag and left it sitting on top of my desk. The leather was stiff enough to conceal the angular outlines of the gun, making it difficult to tell just what it contained. I stared at it, sometimes touching it, as I endured the boring lecture. Needless to say, I avoided doing this whenever Yuko Yoshikawa or Keisuke or anyone else I knew was around. If for any reason one of them were to pick up the pouch, it would create a real problem for me, one that went beyond mere tension and excitement.

I sat by myself in a chair in the smoking area inside the unfamiliar literature department building. Bored, I took the leather pouch out of my bag. There was no one around, maybe because lectures were in session. I was tempted to pull the gun from the pouch, but of course I restrained myself from doing so. I lit a cigarette, and thought about what to do next. I considered calling that girl I'd recently had sex with, but it was more trouble than it was worth.

Just then, I thought about shooting the gun. This wasn't the first time it had occurred to me, but lately I had been thinking about it frequently. The act of firing the gun had always existed within me, and now I realized that, as its presence intensified, my efforts to keep it under control were diminishing. Up until now, I had amused myself with simply the prospect of shooting the gun, but gradually it had taken on a tinge of reality, almost as if I had caused it to proliferate, and it was starting to worry me. Previously, the act of firing the gun had belonged to the potentially distant and uncertain future. Yet, since I had started carrying it around with me, I had the feeling that it was only a question of time. The fact of the matter was that I could use the gun at any time, and it loomed over me as a practical reality that the possibility mounted proportionately with each day. The sight of the gun, the feel of it, evoked a concrete image in my mind of me firing the gun, as if it threatened to break out from within the narrow confines of my fixed imagination, seeking a connection with an actual, physical sensation. The fact that someday I would shoot the gun—I had come to believe that this was an absolute certainty. Being in possession of the gun meant that each day was filled with the potential experience of actually discharging it, and without a doubt there would come a day when I would want to do so—that is to say, I was sure I would fire it. That conviction brought the once-distant future closer, almost as if it had taken on a life of its own, and would compel the first shot to happen. This clearly defined future outcome wanted me to make it materialize, and soon. This demand was gradually intensifying, to the point where it was making me deranged—it had a hold on me, and wouldn't let go. I felt the necessity of it—that I needed to fire it, at least once. Otherwise, this same internal argument would go on forever, and I thought I might just lose my mind.

I had the feeling that firing the gun had begun to shift from a conscious choice to a foregone conclusion without my noticing it. The progression made me a little anxious, and I attempted to think through it carefully, but it made my head hurt and I abandoned the idea. I felt like, regardless of what I came up with, it was already determined anyway. So I decided that it didn't really matter.

My cell phone rang: it was Yuko Yoshikawa. Feeling as

though I had been saved, I answered in a cheerful voice. She told me that she had been asleep, going so far as to yawn loudly, but I didn't believe her. In my mind, she had been with another guy. I thought about it for a moment, then said that it was no big deal, I had some time and just wondered if she wanted to get lunch together. She said that, now that she was awake, she would make her way to campus. She added that she would call when she got here, and then she hung up.

I figured I might as well find a way to kill time while I waited for her. After running through various ideas, I thought I would go to the library and look at newspapers. The news on television was all about what was going on with the U.S. and Afghanistan, and information had dropped off about the dead man who had been found at the Arakawa River. I thought there might be something about it in the newspapers, and that I would be able to peruse several days' worth at the library. And yet, I was a little surprised that this had only first occurred to me as a way of killing time. This ought to have been something I was focused on all along. I had realized as much back when I was in the bathroom at that girl's apartment, and you would have thought that I would be more meticulous about it. For a while I sat there in the smoking area, vacant and motionless. The idea that I might actually be too distracted by the gun was slightly terrifying. I was finely attuned to the gun itself, but not so much to the environment around me. I took notice of a policeman coming my way, but I hadn't thought to make any advance preparations or take preliminary measures. In a panic, I practically ran to the library. Even if the police had shifted their investigation and ruled the Arakawa death a suicide, there was no doubt they would still be trying to determine the whereabouts of the gun. And once the investigation moved in that direction, they would probably start to scrutinize all kinds of people.

I put in a call to Yuko Yoshikawa to push back our plans by an hour, and she said okay. I scanned as many newspapers as I could, focusing on the smaller items while still paying attention to the big stories. The vast majority of the articles were completely irrelevant to me. Whether the Americans had dropped a bomb somewhere in Afghanistan, or whether their strategy would succeed—these kinds of things had nothing to do with me right now. What Japan's reaction would be, or whether Japan would become entangled with it—such questions did not interest me at the moment either. A kid had died after being bullied, and his parents had

sued the school and the bully. There was a fire somewhere, and it was difficult to say whether it had been
arson or an accident. There was a festival. Funds were
embezzled, and the culprit had fled. There was a sci-
entific discovery. Two trucks had collided. Someone
had been run over. An intellectual whose name I didn't
recognize gave his opinion about the United States,
offering advice to the Japanese government. Politicians
quarreled, talking earnestly about something or other.
Two entertainers died. It seemed like the information
I was looking for was not to be found in any of these
newspapers. I continued to leaf through various broad-
sheets, my eyes intently devouring the words. Each day
had been filled with news. Yet it seemed the dead man
by the Arakawa River did not merit a mention. This
project would take time. I kind of regretted not asking
Yuko Yoshikawa for two hours instead of one. But I realized that if I did this every day, it wouldn't take as long
to stay on top of it. I began to tire from the effort of
concentrating, half dragging myself through the task as
I continued to scan the papers.

The article occupied more space than I would have
imagined. It gave me a little shock, literally seeming
to suddenly leap out at me. I had gotten as far as the

newspapers from the 22nd when there it was—the man who had been found near the Arakawa had been identified. His name was Keiichiro Ogiwara, he was 51 years old and had been the manager of an adult entertainment club—everything about him was written right there. Aware that my heart was starting to race, I read through the rest of the article. I could tell that the police were still viewing it as a homicide. The article implied that the club where he had worked was run by people who had ties with organized crime, and went on to suppose that there may have been some kind of financial trouble. In a different paper from the same day, there was another article that said basically the same thing. The only difference was this one said that it wasn't an adult entertainment club; rather, it was a "fashion-health" massage parlor, and one with definite mob ties, that trafficked in prostitution. However, the story hadn't been picked up by any other newspapers, and even in the two where it had run, there were no more articles about it from after that day. Relieved—for the time being, at least—I relocated to the smoking area and lit a cigarette. The cigarette tasted better than usual, and I had to laugh at myself for getting so worked up again.

Nevertheless, I thought over my assumption that the

man had killed himself. When I found him, the man's left hand had been limply stretched up, with his right hand hanging down. And the gun had been lying by his right hand, which was likely his dominant hand. If the man had been shot by someone, would that person have left the gun behind? If the shooter was a gangster, wouldn't that be all the more reason he would need the gun? Otherwise it became evidence, which to him would only be a disadvantage, right? I turned this over in my mind, spinning out conjectures. But it made sense that, not finding the gun at the scene, the police would have no choice but to rule it a homicide. Had they found a suicide note at the man's home? I thought about it but couldn't recall seeing any kind of paper resembling that in the vicinity. It could have been stashed in his breast pocket or something, but then I realized that it must not have been, or the police wouldn't be treating it as a murder. Considering all these things, I seemed to be the one closest to the truth. Obviously, I was the only person who knew that the gun had been at the scene, and that it could have been a suicide. The police were likely confused, and in their confusion, they had probably pared down their investigation. But, I doubted it would go that smoothly. I figured I should avoid making any rash decisions. And I needed to remain aware of these things at all times. I needed to constantly remind myself that this was the situation I was in.

My cell phone rang—it was Yuko Yoshikawa. She mentioned she was hungry a few times, and that she was in the cafeteria, then quickly hung up. I headed for the cafeteria and looked for her, but she wasn't there. For a moment I wondered what had happened, but gave up and just figured I would sit down somewhere. The cafeteria was remarkably empty, so I had no trouble finding a seat. I smoked a cigarette and contemplated the cause of death of the man from the Arakawa River, about gathering information from now on, and about what sort of danger I risked by neglecting to do so.

Someone tapped me on the head, and I turned around to see Yuko Yoshikawa. I complained to her, asking why she always hit me on the head, but she said I deserved it. She had a surly look on her face as she looked back at me. For some reason, I suddenly felt annoyed.

"Come on, you should have looked harder. You give up too easily. I hate that. It gets on my nerves."

"It gets on your nerves? Well, I just figured you must

have gone to the bathroom or something. So I thought the best thing to do would be to sit near the door."

"Hmm, well, when you put it that way, I guess that sounds reasonable, but it still gets on my nerves," she said, and then went on complaining for a while. She was persistent, and I went along with her but soon tired of it. According to her, I was lacking in something. Since I didn't understand what she meant, I listened very closely to what she was saying. The way she saw it, I seemed rather cavalier toward her—apparently I didn't take her seriously enough. I was a little surprised to hear this. I had invited her to lunch, I had gone to the place where we were meeting, and I was consistently talking to her at length. When I said as much to her, she looked me in the eye and made a face as if she were thinking about something.

"You're wrong—well, I guess since you're not my boyfriend, I can't really expect much more than that but—I don't know how to say it, well, this may not come out right but—you're probably like this with everyone. That's how you are—um, I mean, I don't know what it is you're thinking."

"I guess I don't really know either."

"Well, anyhow, I really hate being treated so

dismissively," she said. Then she sat down in a chair and lit a cigarette. "And because of you I've picked up this habit again," she said.

I wasn't sure what she was referring to, but I figured she probably meant smoking, and I gave a little laugh. Then I was seized with the desire to say something clever. "But," I said, "you're probably right, maybe I can be cavalier, but not with you. It may sound strange, but I do act differently depending on who I'm with."

"You're full of it. Isn't that just how you manage to put one over on people?"

"Fine, okay, it doesn't matter."

With that, I cut off the conversation and randomly changed the subject. However, I had a hard time concentrating on anything. She took in what I said and replied in turn, but I wasn't really listening. I thought about how the only way the police could know that I had anything to do with the man from the Arakawa River would be from an eyewitness account—I hadn't seen anyone that night but they might have been there somewhere, and that was how they would know. And if that were the case, I would be in serious trouble. But then again, if that possibility actually existed, wouldn't I already have been approached by the police? I thought about this during my conversation with Yuko. We had lunch, and I sat there with her until evening.

WHEN I RETURNED home to my building, it was completely dark outside, and it had gotten quite chilly. I bought a can of hot coffee from a vending machine next to my building and shook it up as I walked the short distance to my apartment. In that time, I was mostly thinking about Yuko. Today she had again been wearing a short skirt, and when she leaned forward I had seen her pale breasts. I felt satisfied with the way I had behaved today. Tomorrow, I thought, I would ask her out for a drink. But then again, if we ended up doing it, I felt as if the fun would end for me there. I wanted to have sex with her, but once we had done it, I would probably get bored. In my experience so far, that had usually been what happened to me. The anticipation that it would happen again is what made me lose interest. And ultimately—eventually, I thought—it always happened that way, so I quit thinking about it. As I reminded myself, to think too hard about it made doing almost anything impossible. I had found that putting unnecessary emphasis on expectation or supposition rendered me useless. Thinking about all this, I gave a little laugh.

When I had just reached my front door, I heard the sound of a child crying from the apartment next to me. Somehow or other, I was aware that there was a woman and boy of about kindergarten age living there. I often heard the child crying and I always found it annoying, but crying was what kids did, so there wasn't much to be done about it. But now, the crying sounded a little different. This time, I could also hear a woman's screaming coming from that airtight room.

Once inside my own apartment, I could hear two distinct voices even more clearly. I couldn't make out the words, but I could tell that the woman was laughing her head off, and the kid was crying his eyes out. The crying sounded like it poured out from deep within his belly, so loudly that it was a little creepy. I recalled that the boy was quite small, and such a loud cry seemed disproportionate to his size. Aside from the laughing woman, I could also hear a woman yelling, and I was confused. After a little while, though, I figured out that these two voices belonged to the same person.

Eventually I got fed up and put on some music to drown out their voices. It called for something aggressive, so I picked a CD by the German band Rage. As I listened to it, I was reminded of how much I enjoyed hearing music played really loud. Then I took the gun out of the leather pouch, polished it, and carefully put it back in the satchel.

8

I THOUGHT ABOUT where to fire the gun, and decided on somewhere in the mountains. I figured that the area around the mountain that I could see from the window of the train on my way to university would not be dangerous. I didn't know what the mountain was called, but there weren't many houses nearby, and I supposed that, if I went further into the interior of the mountain, the sound wouldn't reach even the ones that were there. Actually, it had occurred to me that, conversely, if I did it in a noisy place, people might not even notice, but I wanted to hear it for myself. The explosive sound the gun made when it discharged its bullets, the corresponding impact transmitted from hand to body, the smoke, the force—I wanted to experience all of these things fully. Thinking about it, I was filled with excitement mixed with nervous tension. I could hardly wait to shoot it, I thought to myself. It was a strange sensation, but it made me happy.

In my lecture, a tall guy in a suit was going on and on about Islamic culture, and then about its history. He was very excited—more intense about it than usual. Come to think of it, I felt like I might have seen him on television once before. But I couldn't be sure whether it had been him, after all, and it had nothing to do with me anyway.

When I left the classroom, Keisuke was waiting for me outside. He was talking about girls and clothes and watches. He said that lately he had seen me with a girl a lot, and asked if she was my girlfriend. I figured he must have been talking about Yuko Yoshikawa. I told him no, but that I was working on it.

"So, I guess you haven't done it yet. But she seems

cute. And quite a body too. You've got an eye for them, don't you? You haven't fallen for her, have you?"

"What do you mean?"

"I just wonder if you're in love with her or something. Cause if you are, I'd have to laugh—how great would it be if you had fallen for some girl? Come on, let's go drinking. You can tell me about it."

"No, you've got the wrong idea. Well, I mean, maybe that's it."

Keisuke seemed to be in a good mood, so I decided to play along with him. He laughed when I pretended to be self-conscious. He tried doggedly to get me to agree to go out drinking with him, but I refused. Today I had been thinking that I would go and scout out the mountain where I had decided to fire the gun. Pragmatically, it wasn't necessary for me to do so, but there were various steps I wanted to put into place before actually shooting it, for the purpose of ensuring my own calm and composure. I had decided to investigate the area around the mountain, to seek out the optimal spot where I should fire it. I thought I would likely derive some pleasure from these preparations.

My phone rang, the call was from my parents' house. A little surprised, I told Keisuke that I had to talk to them. I stood there and answered the phone, then sat down on a nearby bench. Keisuke stayed a short distance away from me for some reason, fumbling to light a cigarette. It was my mother, and again I wondered why she hadn't called the landline in my apartment. If she had something to talk to me about, it seemed like calling there and leaving a message on the machine would be easier. First she asked about my health, and I reassured her that there was nothing to worry about. My mother sounded a little strange—I had thought the same thing when she called the other day. At the time, it had occurred to me that parents and children pick up on these things from each other through the subtlest mannerism or impression. I figured something must have happened at home.

"Is something the matter?" I said. "You don't have to say if you don't want to, but if it's better for me to know about it, then please just tell me. Okay? What is it—it's all right, just go ahead and tell me."

My mother hesitated before saying, "Your father is in critical condition." This made no sense to me, so I asked her to repeat what she had said. The last time I had been at home, my father had been in good health, so I couldn't imagine him sick or in the hospital. We had drunk together, and I had listened to him talk at length about his beloved golf. I asked my mother, hadn't he been fine since then? She fell silent for a moment, then apologized for not knowing how to put it. The person who was in critical condition, she said, was the father to whom I was related by blood.

"Of course, your father and I think of you as our own son. That's only natural—we're parent and child—but, you know, I just couldn't decide what to do, your father and I talked it over and we felt that it was better to tell you, okay, you know, you probably held a grudge against your father—no, not your father who's here, I meant the other one—and I thought it would be best for you—as far as we were concerned—to have forgotten about all that, but then the orphanage contacted us, to say that he was, you know, about to die, and we just couldn't decide what to do, but in the end, we thought we should tell you everything, and then leave it up to you to decide whether or not to go visit him. It must be fifteen years since you've seen him, I bet you wouldn't even recognize him—that's right, you were about six when you became our son. Okay, I'm sorry, you must be surprised, uh, how, you know, I'm sorry, I gave you quite a shock."

My mother rambled on, seeming to break down in

tears midway. I had no idea why she was crying, but her voice choked up and she sounded like she was spilling it all out to me in one breath. I was a little surprised by the suddenness of it, but I had imagined something much worse, so I was sort of relieved. Nevertheless, I grasped that this was a grave scene. And I wondered what would be the best way to respond, as far as my parents were concerned. It was hard to say, but I thought I should probably say that I would go see him, without seeming to worry about it. If I were to state awkwardly that I didn't want to see him, that would seem like I actually did care about it. It might appear as if in my heart I was still holding on to the idea of my real father. But the thought of gleefully going to see him didn't seem right. It was a particularly tricky path between the two. Yet I was aware of an external pressure—though to do what exactly, I wasn't sure.

"Back then, you know, when you came into our family, the people at the orphanage told us that usually in these cases—especially when the actual parent is alive, right—the child's mental condition can be unsettled, and it can take a while for the child to think of you as his parents, so we should take a long view and give you time. Often the child might stop eating meals, or try to run away—even if their birth parent was terrible, they might cry that they want to go back to them. But you—from the beginning, you called us Mother and Father, didn't you—you smiled a lot, you didn't brood on your own, you never cried, we were so happy, you know, we were so glad that you accepted us, but now when I think about it, it seems as if you were just looking out for us—you were such a thoughtful boy, you know, always so kind, weren't you, unusually so for a child—I think you were sensitive to a lot of things."

She broke down midway, and handed the phone over to my father. The first thing he asked me was if I was surprised, and my response was, "Yeah, I guess so." Then he said, "Take your time, give it some thought about whether or not to go see him." Curious as to why he was home at this time of day, I asked him. He was getting close to retirement age, he said, and lately he'd been getting home early.

"If you don't want to go, that's fine, I mean, well, this is all of a sudden, isn't it. Sorry—well, take your time and think about it."

"No, well, I'll go. He's about to die and he wants to see me, right? It doesn't really matter to me either way, but I'll go—honestly, it's kind of annoying. I'm afraid if I don't go, he'll resent me for it. Oh, right, sorry—things are a little tight this month, so . . . I wonder if you could send me ten thousand yen or so. I'm really sorry to ask. When I go out—ah, no, I've got a lot going on, I spent all my money buying a new dictionary."

"You just said you've been going out, huh?" my father said with a little laugh.

"Not at all, that's not what I meant. Really, I'm telling you—but, sorry though—I really need you to send it to me."

"I understand, what else can I do? Make sure you're studying. Oh, and if you do go to see him, I think Mr. Yamane will go with you. I think you'll likely hear from him too."

"Got it. Oh, listen, give Mom a hard time because it seemed like she was crying. Tell her she must be getting sentimental in her old age, okay? Ah, class is about to start," I said and hung up.

I thought about my biological father a little, but in all honesty, the whole thing made no difference to me. I had virtually no memory of the man, so I really didn't harbor any sort of grudge against him. I had heard that the woman he had married had left him and all he had done was drink. And I also remember being told that, for a small child like me, it had been dangerous to live with him when he was in that condition. But as far as I was concerned, that was simply common sense dressed up in other words.

Keisuke had been watching me with concern, but there was nothing to say. In the past, I would have taken this opportunity to tell him that neither of my parents were my real parents, that I had been in an orphanage, and then enjoyed watching his reaction, but of course I didn't do that now. For whatever reason, Keisuke kept trying to be nice to me. He probably guessed something was up from what I had said on the phone.

"All right, then, I'm going to go to that girl's place now," I said, thinking I would leave Keisuke there.

"Huh? Oh, the cute one? What's her name?"

"Ah, not that one—I meant the girl I slept with the other night, go over to her place. And, her name is Yuko. The one you were talking about. Yuko Yoshikawa. I'm just telling you so you'll keep your hands off her."

"What? Why are you going there? I thought you were in love with this one? Hey, what are you doing? Break it off with the other one."

"Come on, nothing wrong with getting what I can, is

there? I mean, I'd rather be with Yuko. I'm serious about her, man."

"Well, then, if you're serious, what else can you do? Guess you'd better go. But you'd better not let Yuko find out."

"Yeah, guess you're right."

FROM THERE, I decided to actually go to that girl's apartment. I didn't have any particular desire to see her, but since I was the one who suggested it, I figured why turn back now? In fact, I often acted according to the idea of "why turn back now?" I searched for the girl's number on my cell phone, then called her. I hadn't known her name, so I had put her in under T for "toast." She answered cheerfully, and when I said I was coming over now, she breezily accepted. She asked if I was hungry, but I said I didn't need to eat. Actually, I wouldn't have minded eating something, but I wanted to see what would happen if I just went there to have sex. There was no reason for it, that's just what I decided to do. I went to her place, and after a brief conversation, she and I had sex. But it didn't go that well at the beginning. At first, I wasn't all that into it, maybe because she didn't feel new and exciting to me. I didn't get fully erect until I was inside her. She moaned a lot, but I kind of doubted it was entirely for real. It made me wonder whether she had actually come, this time as well as the first time we had sex.

Afterward I fell into a dream-filled sleep. Several times, within the dreams, I was aware of the fact that I was dreaming, yet I was unable to control my own actions. When I awoke, just like the last time, the girl was preparing something on the other side of the curtain. I figured it might be toast again, but the only thing she had made was coffee. According to her, I had been asleep for sixteen hours. At first I thought she was making this up, but it was true. The gun sprang to mind, and my eyes hurriedly searched for my bag. But I quickly remembered that I hadn't brought it with me that day. My cell phone rang: it was Yuko Yoshikawa. I hesitated for a moment, then decided to let it ring, waiting for the sound to stop. The girl showed no interest in my behavior. It seemed to take a very long time for the phone to stop ringing.

9

BY THE TIME I left the girl's apartment, it was already getting dark, and I was too exhausted to do anything else. When I said I was leaving, the girl had pressed her body up against mine and thrown me forcefully onto the bed. I let her have her way with me, thinking that she must not have been able to satisfy herself the day before. She liked sex. There probably weren't too many people who disliked it, but she seemed to particularly enjoy it.

I gave up on going to scout out the mountain, aware that I was merely postponing it. Having made that decision, I was terribly relieved that it was still off in the future, and I could feel myself start to relax. Yet this seemed rather strange, because I had thought that I wanted to fire the gun.

As if the act of shooting the gun had taken on a character of its own, the impending realization of this deed loomed over me, and from time to time this awareness gave me the creeps. I had the feeling that this summoning would gradually become unbearable, and that the only way to silence it would be to hurry up and fire it. But I also felt the need to establish some distance. It was in response to this inner awareness that I had come up with the idea of first going to scout out the mountain. But I worried that, when I was up there, the desire to fire the gun might drive me mad. Or rather, that I might be overcome by the reality of shooting it. I lit a cigarette and pondered this for a while. I knew that I wanted to fire the gun, and now I grew curious about where that desire originated. However, there seemed to be no doubt that I wanted to fire it.

I wondered if I might be afraid. Scouting out a place would make me want to shoot it. And if I wanted to shoot it, at some point I definitely would do so. Shooting it once would make me want to shoot it again. I had the feeling that I was afraid of this cycle continuing, that it was this cycle itself that I feared. But just what, I wondered, was the reason for my fear? It couldn't have just been about shooting the gun. Most likely I was afraid of being caught, which was why I was going to check out the mountain first, and I wasn't going to fire the gun unless it was entirely safe to do so. I recalled the excitement I had felt when I first discovered the gun. In the midst of my exhilaration at the time, I had still made an effort to retain a clear awareness. The effort came from trying to keep a certain distance from my own enthusiasm. It felt as though now I was trying to maintain an objective opinion, as I had before, about my part in this process as it took its course. However, it had become more difficult to simply appreciate the feel of the gun without firing it. Once again, I thought about going back. Going back to the time when I discovered it, when it seemed as though we were, I don't know, on equal terms. But that was impossible. The gun was already a part of me—it may have been an exaggeration to say this, but it had penetrated my sense of reason. Firing the gun was in the nature of the gun itself, and it would always motivate me to do so. By making the choice not to shoot it, I felt as if I must choose to return to my former self. Meaning going back to my previous existence, to when I didn't have the gun. Not only would that be difficult, I also found the prospect extremely unpleasant. I could no longer imagine my life without the gun. I now experienced a boundless joy from my daily routine, built around the gun, and it seemed to me that enabling that process would at the same time advance my own development.

When I walked up to my building, I saw the kid from the apartment next to mine. He had a plastic bag in his hand, and he was kicking a small rock as he walked along ahead of me. He had a bruise that looked like a red stain next to his right eye. I figured his mother must have given it to him. He was wearing a gray sweat suit that was a bit grubby, and he was terribly thin. His mother didn't seem to be anywhere around. The boy piqued my interest. Or else it may just have been that I was looking for a distraction.

"Hey, did you buy some candy?"

I made an effort to put a relaxed look on my face as I called out to the kid. Up close, I could see that there was another red bruise in the middle of his forehead, he had a squint, and he gave off a slight stink, which probably came from his overgrown, unkempt hair. My instinct was to turn away to avoid the stench, but I resisted. Using the same calm voice I said, "How did you get those bruises?"

Something strange happened next. The kid cast a glance at me with his out-of-focus eye, and then he threw the plastic bag he was carrying at me and took off running. I was surprised, and I looked back over my shoulder to start running right after him. But the kid was fast, and he was already quite a bit farther away than I had expected. I hesitated for a moment but, thinking that I would look like some kind of criminal chasing after a kid, I let him go. I stood there for a moment, bewildered. Then, in an attempt to settle myself down, I lit a cigarette.

I was about to start walking when I noticed the plastic bag lying in the middle of the street, and I thought about moving it out of the way. But that's when I saw that a crawfish had emerged from the bag on its own. Seeing the crawfish made me feel nostalgic, but as I reached out to touch it, I noticed that it was missing both of its claws. I picked up the bag and looked inside. There were many more crawfish jostling around in it. None of them had their front claws. The many crawfish legs were entangled with each other, and their short arms—the ones without the pincers attached—were moving as if trying to feint an attack. The collective mass seemed as if it formed a single living creature, writhing, appearing to express a uniform rigidity throughout its one body, and producing an odd squeaking sound. Disgusted, I reflexively flung the plastic bag with its red mass away from me. The weighted bottom made a faintly sharp noise when it met the surface of the asphalt. I immediately walked away, but it was a while before I could get the keenness of that sound out of my head.

When I returned to my apartment, the first thing I did was put on some music. But even over the stereo, as if she had been waiting for me, I could hear the woman next door yelling. There was the sound of glass breaking, and some sort of crashing that went on unendingly and with such intensity, it seemed like it might shake the wall itself. After some hesitation, I looked up the phone number for the child welfare office and called. I explained the situation, giving them the address of my building and the number of the apartment next door. The child welfare agent listened intently to what I said. It may have been the agent's manner that made me feel a little better. According to the child welfare agent, this was not the first report of this incident, and they would be able to pay a visit here sometime tomorrow.

I couldn't stand the people who lived next door. I had no interest in listening to that woman's screaming, and I was sick of seeing the kid around. Now I could hear someone crying, but it sounded like the woman. I was starting to get depressed, so I put the gun in the leather pouch and went out. I thought I would just walk around the neighborhood.

I hid the leather pouch in the inside pocket of my coat. I didn't think anyone could tell just by looking at me that I was carrying a gun. My cell phone rang; it was Yuko Yoshikawa. Perfect, I thought, and even though it was already late I invited her to meet me out somewhere. She wavered a bit, but—maybe because of my persistence—eventually she relented. Thinking I would meet up with her near the university, I headed in the direction of the station. At that moment, I recalled the stink coming off the kid, and I felt a little nauseated.

10

IT WAS DEFINITELY the first time I had been to the university at night. The orange glow of the outdoor lights shone on the surroundings, and cast the buildings in a dim ochre silhouette. Light came from several windows, suggesting that there were still people inside. I assumed they were gathered for some kind of activity or group; there were people around outside as well, some of them couples with arms linked. For whatever reason, Yuko Yoshikawa had said that she wanted to walk around campus. I'd tried to get her to go somewhere for a drink, but she said that she felt like being somewhere quiet. I bought two cans of hot coffee from a vending machine and handed one to Yuko. She thanked me, although she seemed sort of depressed. I asked her repeatedly what was wrong, but she wouldn't tell me. I got tired of asking, and decided to light a cigarette. As I nonchalantly brushed over the outside of my jacket where the gun was, I thought about what we might do now.

She spoke at last. "I'm sorry. I guess I'm not much company tonight. I don't know, I can't really put in into words, but sometimes I get like this. For no reason, just, you know? But it's good for me to be with someone. I don't like to let anyone see me when I'm like this but, well, I didn't want to be alone. I'm not even sure what I'm talking about, but hey, thanks."

She popped the tab on the coffee I had given her and took a sip.

"No, I'm the one who invited you out, right?—some friends were going out drinking, and they had their girlfriends with them, so I just thought, if you were free—but, no, it's fine. I don't really feel like drinking either."

"What? Are you sure? You mean, you were with them? Are you sure it's all right?"

"Don't worry about it—when I heard your voice, I could tell something was wrong, so I decided to change my plans."

"But what about seeing them?"

"It's fine—they're with their girlfriends, they can drink with them."

I was a little disappointed that she was wearing jeans. Again I wondered about what to do now, then decided that we shouldn't do anything. As I looked over her hair, which grazed her shoulders, her wide eyes, and her breasts, whose outline I could still make out through her sweatshirt, I imagined having sex with her. But because I had decided to take my time getting there, I tried as best I could to direct my attention elsewhere. Even though it didn't really seem to matter, I figured I would keep trying to take it slow.

"What about your boyfriend, can't you talk to him about it?"

"Boyfriend? I don't have one. Not even."

"You don't? Come on, don't lie."

"I'm not lying. I mean, I don't need anyone right now. I'm sick of it. I'm done. I don't need anyone anymore. It seems like a waste of time. I mean, I feel worn out, and like, guys just don't understand."

"Worn out? Really? But I guess I know what you mean."

"No, you don't. Sorry, but that's just how I feel. Still, I can't stand it. I don't need anyone right now—I don't need the trouble, I don't need the ridiculousness."

"Hmm, did something happen? I mean, you don't have to talk about it, if you don't want to."

"No, nothing in particular. I think it happens all the time, this kind of thing. Happens all the time, but I mean, it just gets to me, you know? It's absurd," she said, and laughed to herself.

She really did seem like she was down. Nevertheless I found myself in a very interesting position. Gauging her mood, and then trying to delve deeper into her thoughts, was a challenge, and that's what made it interesting for me. I had the impression that, from a distance, we must have looked like a couple talking about something serious. And I bet that nobody would have thought that I had a gun stashed inside my coat.

I soon realized that I was feeling extremely drowsy. It happened without any warning, coming over me suddenly like a veil. The orange lights grew blurry, and I couldn't understand everything Yuko was saying. Trying

to remain awake, I drank my coffee, and stood up forcefully. I asked if she wanted to walk a little.

Instead of replying to me, she said, "I feel like I don't
know what's wrong with me."

"What do you mean?"

"Ugh, it's nothing. Just that, I feel strange today. Sorry.
I can't stop apologizing."

"I'm the one who should apologize."

"For what?"

"Hmm?" I was so sleepy, I don't know how many times
I stifled a yawn. "Anyway, this kind of thing happens, I
mean, no matter what you do, sometimes you feel bad.
So don't worry about it." My head felt muddled, and I
couldn't quite grasp the words I wanted to say. I headed
for the vending machine again, this time buying an iced
black coffee. I went to the bathroom and splashed water
on my face. Yuko eyed me, repeatedly asking if I was
okay. I couldn't think of an appropriate response, so I
just tried to laugh it off.

"Hey, it's kind of cold," she said. "Do you want to
come to my place? It's a mess but . . ."

"What do you mean?"

"I mean, it's getting cold out, and well . . . my apartment is near here." She looked at me as she spoke.

I hesitated a little—I wanted to say something clever in response. I was a little nervous thinking about how she might react, and I enjoyed the feeling. I put on a troubled look, and told her that I would take a pass.

"I don't think I could control myself, if we went to your apartment. I'm weak, you know. And with you in a fragile state, I mean, I might try to take advantage. Cowardly, aren't I? That's what I mean. Maybe you should reconsider. I'd like to think I wouldn't be like other guys, that I could take care of you. I get the feeling you know what you're saying, but still, this is serious. That's why, well, think about it. When you're feeling better. You can let me know anytime."

I looked at her as I finished speaking, and she seemed to be a little taken aback. The expression on her face gave me a feeling of satisfaction. She said something briefly, but so softly that I couldn't really hear her. I was worried that my face may have revealed my glee, which for whatever reason I didn't want her to see, so I had looked away mid-sentence. She grasped my hand and leaned into me as we started walking again. I was again overcome with drowsiness; it took effort for me to remain alert.

As we descended a stone staircase, she chattered

away randomly. About how she couldn't abide cheating, about places she wished she could travel to—those kinds of things. Struggling through my stupor, I managed to smile and respond to her. When we reached the bottom of the stairs, suddenly she pressed her body against mine. I was a little caught off guard, but I didn't lose my balance. She put her arms around me, so I put mine around her. At that moment, I caught the scent of her hair. There was something familiar about it, yet for some reason, I felt uneasy. As that uneasiness gradually spread throughout my body, it seemed to make me forget all about my drowsiness. I felt a dull ache in my heart, and I was seized with an inexplicable desire to flee—the sensation seemed to take my breath away. Dazedly, I just kept holding her in my arms. As I stood there, I felt the oddest sensation—I can't really describe it—as if I were in limbo and I couldn't move.

"I feel like," she started to say, and apparently she was already in tears. "Sometimes, I just feel like crying. I don't know why, all these feelings well up inside. But, right now, I guess I feel better. No doubt you'll see this side of me again, but hey, thanks."

I nodded, but I wasn't really thinking about anything. Then I walked her back to the building where she lived, and left her there, hoping it wasn't too awkward. Along the way, for some reason, I broke into a run. As I ran, the gun in my jacket jostled up and down. Each time it did so, the gun struck up against my left lower torso. It hurt, but I didn't do anything about it. In an attempt to calm myself down, I stopped and smoked a cigarette, inhaling repeatedly as I mindlessly ran my hand over the leather pouch that contained the gun.

I TOOK THE train, getting off at the station near my building. The entire time, I never let go of the leather pouch, reassuring myself of its weight, occasionally putting my hand inside the pouch and touching the gun itself. My mind was almost completely blank. I just kept touching the gun, making sure that it was at my side.

I took the gun out of the leather pouch and put it directly in my jacket pocket. Within the pocket, I gripped the gun, relishing the feel of it there. Something about that action was incredibly reassuring to me. The metal of the gun was cool—no matter how much I handled it, it still didn't warm up—and yet it felt like a part of me. I had put my finger on the trigger, but the trigger offered up its own resistance. I worried that the gun might fire even without the hammer being lowered, so I stopped fingering the trigger. At that moment, I realized that I still didn't know much about the gun. The thought saddened me for some reason, yet I did not release my grip. It seemed as though I had never held onto anything so tightly in my life. I squeezed my hand even more firmly, as if I wanted the gun to like me, but the gun showed no reaction. This was to be expected, and yet for some reason it pained me. Nevertheless, I felt the gun remain at my side.

I went up the stairs to the pedestrian bridge, walking across it slowly as I looked down on the street below. The path on the bridge was enclosed on both sides with plastic fencing, obscuring me from view from the waist down. So I took the gun out from my pocket and walked along with it in my hand. It made no difference, but I carried it all the way to stairs on the other end, where I put it away, and it gave me a little jolt of satisfaction. I walked slowly, and when I could see my building, I turned and went in the opposite direction. For some reason, I had no interest in going home. I don't know why, but that was very clear to me. I bought a hot coffee from a vending machine and, as I drank it, I figured I would walk around until I was tired. I felt like I was in a daze, but not from drowsiness—this time it seemed like something different. I walked slowly though the hushed and darkened streets, gripping the gun inside my pocket. I passed through a residential area, then went over the railway tracks at a crossing and walked along a street beside a park.

At that moment I heard a sound, like the grass rubbing intensely against itself. I thought it could have been a cat or a dog running through a clump of bushes, but the simple thought occurred to me that it might be another dead body. I had nothing else to do, so I headed to the other side of the park fence where I had heard the sound coming from. If it was another dead body, I might find a second gun, but the idea didn't really interest me. This gun was enough for me—the fact was, I didn't need another gun. As I was walking I thought, there was no way I would just happen upon another dead body, and I laughed to myself a little. And, if it was a dead body, there was no reason to think it would have made a noise.

I went over the fence and entered the small park. It was pretty typical, with swings and a slide. I could still hear the sound. I walked around, and realized that I had passed where it was coming from. Just in front of the fence, a part of the rough and overgrown bushes was moving slightly. The sound was coming from there. It gave me the creeps, but I had come this far, and I was curious to know what was making that noise. I approached slowly, trying to determine what was moving within the grass. I was a little nervous, but it was nothing compared to the intensity of how I felt before, when I approached the man lying by the Arakawa River. Based on the way it was moving, I tried to imagine what could be in the grass. Trying hard to pay attention, I moved closer and gripped the gun in my pocket, just in case.

The first thing I saw was a black clump. The clump was writhing and twitching violently, while still attempting to stand on its feet. It took a while for me to realize that it was a black cat—at first all I could do was just stare at it uncomprehendingly. The wet fur along the cat's spine reflected the light from the streetlamp, and the white line that shone there was so bright it almost hurt my eyes. It also took me a while to realize that the wetness along its spine was blood. The grass near the black cat was matted down, perhaps from its writhing, and the surrounding weeds had formed a sort of depression in a small space that encircled the cat. Looking closer, I saw the black cat was in the center of a pool of blood—it was all over everything, even at my feet where I was standing two meters away. I was surprised by how much blood there was, yet more than anything, I was transfixed by the sight of the cat's violent convulsions— I couldn't look away. Its head and forepaws were down on the grass, and it was straining to stand up with its hind legs. Then, the convulsions that began at the nape of its neck and continued along its spine would extend to the rest of the cat's body, causing it to shake intensely and irregularly in every direction. The black cat's neck was on the ground at a strange angle, and the way it was bent made it seem as though the cat would no longer be able to stand up normally. I recoiled, thinking I wanted to get away, but for some reason I couldn't bring myself to leave, and I just stood there watching the spectacle. The black cat coughed up something, and there was blood mixed in with whatever filth came out. In the pool of blood around the cat, I caught sight of what looked like fragments of crawfish shells, which took me a little by surprise. The crawfish made me think of that kid, connecting them in my mind. For a moment, I thought the kid might have done this, but that was hard to imagine. He was still pretty small, and there was no way he could have caused such injury to this cat. The black cat must have eaten these crawfish in a pond or marsh somewhere, and here were the remnants. Or maybe the cat had eaten that mass of crawfish that were missing claws after I had tossed it aside the other day. I figured this cat must have been run over by a car, or maybe some junior high student had injured it, and I wished I hadn't seen it. And yet, the fact that I had seen it made me feel as though I was now inevitably entangled with this black cat.

Just then, something bizarre happened. With its head as a pivot on the ground, the black cat moved its hind legs slowly and started turning, as if drawing a circle around the spot. I gasped—I could do nothing but stare at such a display of futile motion, as if the cat were abandoned to instinct. But that movement brought the front of the cat's head in my direction. Not surprisingly, I found myself staring it in the face. The black cat's gleaming eyes were both open wide, its mouth contorted into a strange shape—its face was filled with such agony, its expression even looked human. At that moment, the black cat let out a little cry. It repeated the sound three more times, calling out to me. I was listening to its cry for I don't know how long, and the whole time, a single thought kept running through my mind. I surveyed the area, and after making sure no one was there, I looked around again. But this second glance wasn't meant to check on my immediate surroundings; what I was looking at was the row of three darkened houses in the distance, as well as the utility pole next to them, the street, the tree towering behind me, the parked white van, the area around the slide, the sky and where it verged with several angular buildings, the grass, the white fence, and so on. However, in this series of movements, I didn't see a single soul. I was sweating, my arms were numb, and my legs felt disturbingly unstable. The expression on the black cat's face was too creepy; the cat made no effort to look at anything other than me. I kept hearing the cat's cry, but I was gradually overcome with the delusion that it was coming from within my own head, and then my mind went blank. I pulled the gun out from my pocket, though it didn't feel like I was moving on my own. Lodged in my pocket, my right hand had been damp with perspiration, and I felt an immediate chill as it met the outside air. Out in the open, the gun seemed to take on more of a presence and grow heavier, at the same time appearing even more beautiful to me. I extended my right hand out in front of me and pointed the barrel of the gun at the black cat, but I still didn't think I would fire it. All I wanted was to assume that position—I remained rigid in the pose. Then I slowly cocked the hammer. It was heavier than I had imagined; it took strength to lower it. Once it was cocked, with a metallic clink the trigger moved ever so slightly toward me. When I saw this, I thought that it might fire just from cocking the hammer, but the trigger stopped there. The rest of the effort was left to my index finger. I felt an ache in my chest; I heard my own heart beating. It was such a strange sound, I didn't think it could possibly be coming from me. I faced the black cat, and in my mind, I said to it, *Stay right there.* It was clearly frightened but, I thought, it wanted to be out of its misery. Still facing me, the black cat didn't move. At that moment I had the impression that, somehow, the cat understood precisely what I was about to do. The feeling had come over me that the gun and I had become one. My entire being had become an extension of the gun. The full-body sensation of merging with this overwhelming presence, with the palpable intention of this gun, filled me with an exhilaration that I had never before experienced. Yet at the same time, I also noticed a presence within me that would interfere with it. That resistance wanted to stop me somehow. But it seemed like too much trouble to give it my full attention and—as if to skip over the thought process yet without mentally preparing myself for the moment of firing—I squeezed the trigger. There was a fiercely explosive sound that echoed throughout the hushed silence, and at that moment, I saw a violet flame escape the barrel. A plume of gray smoke burst forth, and an intense reverberating shock ran up my arm. I had expected it, but it was so strong that it knocked me off balance. The black clump rolled over, splattering fluid as it appeared to be blown to bits. I had imagined that it would leave a hole in the black cat, but the reality was that the bullet had gouged out its body like an explosion. The first thing I was aware of thinking was, *That was a direct hit*. And right away I had the desire to experience the sensation that went along with that action again. I cocked the hammer once more, aimed at the black clump, and squeezed the trigger a second time. The same impact as before had already transformed into an intoxicating pleasure. Within that, my original intention—to put an end to the black cat's suffering—had vanished. The bullet may have only grazed it, because this time the clump didn't roll away, it stayed in the same place, only changing shape. The smell of gunpowder had reached my nostrils, and I could almost taste the numbness that was left in my arms. Then I looked around me, as if something had attracted my notice, and as I made sure no one was there, I cowered with an unfamiliar fear, almost dropping the gun. Realizing that I needed to hurry up and get out of there, I put the gun in my pocket and started off at a half-run. Aware of the excitement welling up inside me, yet thinking only of getting away from there, midway I broke into a full sprint. I had no idea what I was running past—I didn't care, I just ran. It took a while for me to realize that running made me even more conspicuous. I became intensely anxious, worrying that someone might have seen me, yet the anxiety was surpassed by the joy I felt at the same time. It occurred to me that I was not the person I used to be. You could say that I had discovered a supreme joy, and I savored it. I felt grateful to the gun for enabling me to experience this, and I knew I would do anything for it. I had no doubt that this thing I felt was love. I wanted to get back to my apartment and polish the gun thoroughly, as soon as I could. Filled with the joy that spontaneously rose up within me, I wanted to affirm everything in this world. I felt happiness—a happiness that I thought would last until the day I died.

11

THE INSIDE OF the hospital reeked of antiseptic. The orphanage director walking alongside me had shrunken into old man. When I had been at the orphanage, he had still been spry in his middle age. When he first saw me again, he had smiled and embraced me happily, saying, "You've grown." Then he asked me in detail about university, about my family, about my life. I answered each question in turn, but, maybe because of the stench of the antiseptic, I grew irritable. He talked a lot about me when I was little. About how—for a child at the orphanage—I had caused surprisingly few problems, about how I did what I was told, about how I studied hard—he spoke without pausing; I couldn't get a word in edgewise. Then, just as I expected, he said, "But that was exactly why, on the contrary, I was worried about you." He went on, "Though seeing you now, there was no need to worry."

I told him I wanted to smoke a cigarette, although quite a long time had elapsed from when I had first wanted to say so until I was able to. "Good idea," he said, "let's take a little break," and he led me to the hospital cafeteria. All I wanted was a smoke, but he offered me something to drink, so I asked for coffee. He ordered the same thing, and like me he lit a cigarette. Boy, he said, I was all grown up now; time really did fly.

"But, well, the person you're about to see is your father, so you must be nervous. I know it's really none of my business, but I think that later on, when you're older, you would probably have regretted not seeing him. I wanted you to know about him, so when I heard you were coming, honestly, I was relieved and happy."

"Is he really in critical condition?"

"Oh, they say it won't be long now. He has cancer

of the liver, you know. It's already spread to his throat, that's what the doctor at the hospital was saying. Even your father knows this. He's conscious, but only just barely, you know, and he keeps repeating that he wants to see you."

"But I wonder, why does he want to see me?"

"Oh, I can understand how you must feel, but I bet that, staring death in the face, he must want to apologize for things. I think I can understand that too. Lately, there are times when the faces of those I want to say I'm sorry to flicker through my mind."

"You're all right, aren't you?"

"Oh no, I'm fine, but I did some terrible things when I was young, too. It's just that, when I look back, there are stories I'm ashamed of."

I wanted to hurry up and get this over with. Ever since firing the gun, I had felt elated, and my general mood had been similarly improved. As far as I was concerned, going to the hospital meant killing my own buzz. I didn't want to get involved with unnecessary things. I had used up two of the bullets the other night, and now I had to think about how I would get more bullets when I needed them. I also needed to consider whether anyone had actually seen me that night. I had a lot of things to do. I saw no reason to let someone I was merely related to by blood get in the way of all that. Wanting to deal with it quickly, I proposed to the director that we get going, then considered it further, and thought to add that I was anxious to see the man. The director nodded, and paid the bill. He suggested that it might be best for me to go in and see him on my own. "I'll just wait somewhere," he said.

The door was white, and the area near it was quiet. I opened the door, and as promised, the director made no attempt to enter, he simply nodded at me. I had known he would nod, so seeing him do so was satisfying somehow. The room was cramped, with three beds lined up in the center of it. Each bed had an IV drip attached, and various tubes extending off it; I felt as though I had stepped into some kind of laboratory. The white curtain over the window had been left closed, and there was a scrawny arrangement of sorry-looking flowers near it on a stand. The apparatus by the bed in the middle was larger than those by the other two, and seemed like it must have been expensive. I approached the bed that was closest to me, and looked down on the man who was lying there. He looked like an ordinary, unremarkable old man. His eyes were closed as if he were sleeping, and he was covered in wrinkles—he reminded me of a mummy. I had a hard time imagining that this person was my father, but what did I expect? I remembered the time long ago, when I learned about DNA on the television at the orphanage. It had given me a serious shock. I had thought that the idea of bloodlines was more like a kind of superstition or something, but DNA gave it the ring of truth, and I had to admit that heredity was an established fact. Biologically half of me was made up of genes from that bastard, and the other half from some woman I'd never known, who had disappeared. The realization had caused me to lose interest in myself. It was better not to engage in introspection or self-awareness; in order to go on with my life, I sort of shut down, in a childlike way. I reminded myself that I didn't need to think about it; I had bummed myself out a little, but I quickly got over it.

I was conscious of the gun, and then I remembered that I had left it at my apartment that day. It wasn't like I thought if I had it with me I might shoot my father, but I had the feeling it was better that I hadn't brought it. To me, it seemed a shame for the precious gun to be in the presence of my father. In fact, as soon as I entered the room, I was glad I didn't have it. The air was stuffy, the mood somber. It didn't fit with the nature of the gun, which was much better suited to my apartment or the crisp air of the park that night.

The IV was filled with a dull yellow fluid, which passed through a translucent tube and was being infused into the man's body. I became intrigued by the idea of what would happen to him if I were to yank this out. His eyes would probably pop open as he stared at me in surprise. It would likely create a scene. A son with a grudge pays a visit to his father and takes his life. I thought it would make quite a fascinating story for the public. But I wasn't about to do that. I had no interest in this man, and resentment was one of several emotions that I didn't really comprehend. It made no difference to me. I didn't care if he died right here, or if he recovered and lived a happy life.

I stared at the white seal that was stuck on the IV, and noticed that the name written on it said Mr. Nishioka. I had no memory of that name. Realizing that I was standing over the wrong man, I chuckled to myself a little. Yet I felt as though I had already done what I had intended, and I thought about just going home. I was about to leave, but since I had come this far, I reconsidered, figuring I would just spend a little time with him, and approached another bed. I saw the name I recognized, and as I had done before, I looked down over the proprietor of this IV. This man was incredibly dark-skinned. His gray-flecked hair was receding, and something about it struck me as undignified. The man appeared to be awake; his eyes were wide open and fixed on me. With a slight tremor of his lips as though he wanted to say something, he peered intently, his gaze unwavering. Watching his eyes grow red, I got more and more fed up, yet at the same time, I found it amusing. There was something indescribable about the way he displayed such a classic reaction. His right arm trembled as it moved, but maybe because it was so leathery, I had no interest in catching hold of it. His voice so hoarse it sounded like an exhalation, he called out my name, "Toru?" Thinking about how funny it would be if I denied it, I slowly moved my head from left to right. But he seemed to have misunderstood, and the tears flowed even more as he muttered, "Aha, aha." I was unsure of what to do; I had the urge to blame him for something— maybe for not being asleep. Again he moved his right arm slightly, but I still couldn't bring myself to grasp it.

The sound of the man's labored breathing seemed to cling to my ears. I could only stand there, rooted to the spot, looking down over him. There was nothing else for me to do, so I thought about just going home. But the man was working hard to open his mouth, trying again to say something. As I stared at the thickness of those two dark red lips, I continued to wonder why I had come here, after all this time. And moreover, why did I still feel an external pressure, as if there were something here I needed to do? I didn't quite understand what that was about, but it didn't seem all that complicated. Just then, I heard the man say in the same hoarse voice, "Can you forgive me?" I nearly burst into laughter, the boredom of a moment ago seemingly unreal, and I almost let out an awkward noise. There was something indescribably funny about how, in the face of death, he spouted such a melodramatic and trite line. I figured he must have seen a scene like this in a television show or a movie. But he was serious. His emotionally charged earnest-ness seemed curiously exaggerated. An idea occurred to me that made me grab his right hand. "I don't care about that," I said to him. "Just hurry up and get better," I went on. As I spoke the words, I did a relatively good job of stifling my laughter. I'm sure if I had called him Father it would have been perfect, but for some reason I resisted. As he wept, he tried to bring his face closer to my hand.

Something about this gesture made me think of a baby, and in that moment, I pulled my hand away. As soon as I had felt the tears from this man's eyes on my own skin, my hand had recoiled as if it had a mind of its own. A chill ran through my body, and even though I knew it was an overreaction, it gave me the creeps. The man looked at me, flummoxed, and for some reason, I smiled back at him. I knew that wasn't necessary, but I may have been trying to counteract his infantile creepiness, and I smirked with contempt as I looked down over him triumphantly. I thought about letting my saliva dribble onto his face, but of course I didn't do that. However, I had looked at him for about as long as I could stand to, and I felt like I had done what I had come for. So I said, "I'm not Toru." And then, "Wrong person, sorry," and I left the room.

Out in the corridor, the man from the orphanage looked at me with concern. I was surprised to find him still here, but when I thought about it, I had to admit it was perfectly natural. "How did it go?" he asked, trying to gauge my state. The way that he asked irritated me, but on second thought, that too was a perfectly natural thing to ask. I hesitated for a moment. "We don't look anything like each other," I said, when in fact, his eyes and the shape of his nose had looked disturbingly familiar. "Uh-huh, but . . . Well, I guess I shouldn't have bothered you," he said, turning to me with an even more concerned expression. I told myself that what he had done had been out of the kindness of his heart, and I forced myself to tough it out.

I CALLED THE toast girl, and went to her apartment. As I entered her from behind, I grabbed her hair and drew her body toward me. She was breathing very heavily, but while we were at it, things seemed to get awkward. In the same position, I ran my tongue along the side of her neck and sucked lustily. She started complaining that her boyfriend would notice, but even though I wasn't all that into it anyway, I kept doing it over and over again. The whole time, I felt like I might fall asleep. For some reason, I started to get annoyed, so I figured I'd better come quickly, and I focused on that.

Afterward I did sleep, and woke up in the middle of the night. The girl seemed exhausted—maybe I had worn her out—and was sound asleep, breathing peacefully. I wrote a perfunctory note, left her apartment, and took a taxi home to my own place. After I got back there, I still felt pretty tired, and when I awoke, it was fifteen hours later. I may have slept too much, because I could feel an ache behind my eyes, yet I might have kept on sleeping for who knows how much longer. Then I remembered something from when I was little. I couldn't be sure whether I remembered it from a dream, or if it happened when I was awake, but I pondered it idly. When I was at the orphanage, I had told myself that if I didn't think about things, then I wouldn't be unhappy. Even if I had already been visited by misfortune, so long as I was unaware of it, or didn't think about it, the unhappiness could not materialize. I had realized this, and put it into practice. The orphanage was in a small white building. There was a piano, and stuffed animals, and a television. There was no outdoor space, but we had a soccer ball and baseball equipment. More and more memories seemed ready to flow out of me, if I had chosen to let them free.

12

WHAT WOKE ME up was the sound of the front door bell. It echoed sharply within my tiny apartment, loud enough to awaken me. I intended to ignore it, and reeled in my bedding that had been cast aside, but the sound rang out once more. Fed up, I got out of bed and lit a cigarette. I waited for whomever it was to give up, but the doorbell sounded again, and this time I also heard pounding on the door. Nothing to be done about it; I put out my cigarette and looked through the peephole to see who was there. It was a man I didn't recognize. He was probably soliciting or canvassing, but something about him gave me a strange impression. He was middle-aged, short with black hair. He looked like an ordinary guy, but he had a certain overbearing quality. He banged on the door again and, because I was so close this time, it startled me. I opened the door, and he said to me, "Were you sleeping?" and "I'm sorry about that." He was smiling, but his narrowed eyes were looking at me the whole time. This pissed me off, but I didn't know what it meant. Then he said, "I'm a policeman," and showed me his badge in a black case.

"Ah, I apologize for disturbing you, but I'd like to ask you about something. Is now a good time?"

He smiled as he spoke, as if he was trying to reassure me, but there was something calculating in his look. I was taut with anxiety; my mind went blank for a moment. My heart began to race, and I could feel sweat start to break out on my face. I tried not to let it show, telling myself to keep it together. But his eyes remained focused on mine. Unable to hold the man's gaze, I looked away.

"No, I'm just surprised. It's so out of the blue . . . Wow, it's like on TV, I mean, you really show your badge

and everything . . . Oh, sorry. Uh . . . What is it? I was
sleeping," I said, smiling as I looked at the man.

"Oh," he said, "it's nothing really." But I didn't believe
him. In my head, I said to myself over and over, *You
really don't know anything, the police have nothing to do
with you.*

"Well, the other day, a stray cat—ah, it's a terrible
story—it was found dead and covered in blood, you see.
In the park over there. The park is pretty close to where
you live. To think there's someone out there who did this
really awful thing—it's just that I have a cat myself—
well, that's not really the point, no, no, I'm getting away
from the story. Now, the thing is, I'm going around
the neighborhood, calling on people like this, to see
whether you might know something about it. That . . .
incident . . . do you know anything?" He smiled again
as he looked at me.

I managed to listen calmly to his story. I was a little
surprised by my own behavior, but at the same time, I
felt like I would be able to make it through this. However, I would have to be sure to choose my words pru-
dently. Trying to avoid looking at the man, I nodded several times.

"Wow, that's terrible, but why are the police

investigating something like this? Ah, I mean, please excuse me for asking, I mean, sorry, I don't know anything. But I'd like to help."

"Oh, well, that's not what I'm investigating," the man said with a curt laugh. "The problem is, we retrieved a bullet from the cat's body. It's a shell—the real thing, .357-caliber magnum. That's powerful. What's more, it's not the kind of gun that's widely available in Japan. Really, it's quite rare. Which means that, whoever did this to the cat must have the gun, right? This is a serious incident. And in such a quiet residential neighborhood. What do you think? Now it's not so unusual that the police are involved, is it?"

"I see, that's horrible. I hope you catch the person soon."

Conscious of maintaining an expression of mild surprise, I looked the man in the face. Anyone in Japan would likely be a little shocked when they heard the word "gun." He was studying my face seriously; I could tell that he was trying to read even the slightest shift that registered there. He hastily flashed a smile, as if noticing his own behavior, but the whole thing seemed like an act to me. I had the feeling this guy was convinced of my involvement, and for a moment I was seized with fear, but I knew that I could still keep my cool. So, with feigned detachment but full attention, I waited for what he would say next.

"Do you have a white jacket?"

"What do you mean?"

"A white jacket, you see. A white jacket, about hip length. Do you have one?"

"I do but . . ." As I said this, I felt a dull thud in my heart.

"We have someone who heard something that sounded like gunshots that night. Using that date, we could determine when the cat died. And on that day, we have someone who saw a young man wearing a white jacket running near there. The guy who witnessed this works as a clerk in a convenience store. No one wears a jacket like that to go jogging. And, he said that there was something strange about the young man. He said he seemed, you know, very happy. The clerk knew who you were. He said you come into the store often. It would seem that . . . that might have been you."

"But, how did he know my address . . . ?"

"The parcel delivery service. The same clerk works the convenience store's parcel delivery service. The sender's address is clearly specified. The store keeps a duplicate copy on file, in case something goes wrong with the delivery. You used it once to try to send your parents a picture frame. Such a good son, was it for their anniversary or something? But because of the store's error, it got broken. But you—and I was a little surprised when I heard this—he said you didn't get angry. On the contrary, you never even looked upset. You never even claimed the amount of the damages—nothing. The clerk who is the eyewitness, he is the person who dropped it. He remembered what happened very clearly. And yet, to this day, you still come in to buy things at the store that was at fault. The clerk knows you. He knows your face, and he also knows the clothes that you usually wear."

This time, the man wore a different smile than before. It was difficult to keep my cool. But I knew this still wasn't enough to connect me with the gun.

"When was this? The day the cat was shot. There was definitely a time recently when I was running through the neighborhood. I needed to get back to my apartment right away."

"Really? What for?"

"Do I really need to say?"

"Yes, for reference."

I thought a moment, then said, "A girl was waiting for

me in my apartment. She was making dinner, but I was running late, so I needed to get home quickly," I went on. But the man seemed uninterested in my story. His attitude surprised me, since he had been the one to ask me why I had been running.

"Ah, I see," he said. "Well, then. That doesn't really concern me. Not at all. There's just one thing, perhaps you can tell me. I just can't seem to get it off my mind. At the time, why were you running with your right hand in your pocket? Hardly anyone runs with their hands in their pockets, do they? And why were you so happy? That's what the store clerk said. That you seemed extremely happy. Happy, and yet, sweating profusely."

The man fell silent, and I realized that it was now my turn to speak.

"That's no big deal, is it? I don't really remember, but if I happened to think about something funny, that's probably why I was laughing, and I always sweat when I run. I can't really say. As for my hand being in my pocket, I don't really remember that either, but there was probably something inside it—like my cell phone—that I didn't want to fall out. I don't know."

The man took out a cigarette and lit it while I was saying this. I could tell that he intended for this conversation to go on for a while, so I said, "I'm busy right now."

But he ignored me. As if to himself, he said, "Hmm, that's interesting." Then he said to me, "Look, uh, why talk about this here? Your neighbors can see us, right? Why don't you let me inside for a minute—sorry, but it's getting a little cold."

"No, I'm sorry, but I don't think so. It's a mess, and I'm really not comfortable letting a complete stranger into my apartment. I don't think that's so unusual."

"I'm a detective. I'm not going to steal anything."

"No, it's not that I suspect you would, but I simply prefer not to. And, if you'll forgive me for saying so, it's a pretty vague excuse for trying to invite yourself into my apartment. I think for most people, it's normal not to want to be involved with the police, isn't it? Would you please leave now? I'm starting to get angry."

"Hey, take it easy, just another minute—please listen to what else I have to say," he said, taking a drag on his cigarette. "In normal situations, at this point I usually just leave. When the person gets annoyed, it makes things difficult. But this time, I can't do that. Because a gun is involved, there's no time to lose. This can't wait until tomorrow. In just one day, something terrible can happen. That's the truth. I've seen these cases too many times. I don't want to regret this later. You know about the Arakawa River incident, right?"

"What?"

"I'm talking about the man who was found murdered by the Arakawa River. You're familiar with it, aren't you?"

I could feel the man's eyes on me as I tried to contain my growing nervousness. So I gazed back at him, first with a look as if I were trying to recall something, then with an expression conveying puzzlement at what he was saying.

"I saw it on television, but what is that about?"

"The bullet that man was shot in the head with and the bullet that was retrieved from the cat's body are the same type."

"Oh, is that so? You mean . . . No way, come on! You think someone murdered that cat?"

"Ah, well, listen to what I have to say. This won't take much longer," he said, stamping out the cigarette he had dropped on the ground and lighting a new one. I still had the feeling that, as he did so, he was gauging the state I was in. When he'd suddenly brought up the Arakawa murder just now, I suspected that had been his intention all along.

"Would you mind if we moved to a coffee shop or someplace? I doubt you would agree to come down for questioning voluntarily—and that wouldn't really work for me, either. But if you refuse now, I'll come back again tomorrow, and I'll go to your school as well. So wouldn't it be easier just to dispel any suspicion right here and now?"

He said this to me and then, without waiting for my response, he continued, "I'll wait a few minutes while you get dressed."

UNFORTUNATELY, THERE WAS nothing I could do but go with the man to the coffee shop. I felt an almost paroxysmal urge to shoot him with the gun, but I knew what it would mean for me if I did. I closed the door and put the gun in the back of the closet, in case something happened. If he came inside the apartment, I figured he would probably find it anyway, but I didn't have much time. Then again, he still didn't have any definitive proof that the gun was in my possession. And without evidence, there was no reason to think that he would be able to search my apartment. And, when I thought about it, there shouldn't be any such evidence. If that scanty eyewitness testimony was the only thing they had against me, then I found it hard to imagine that it would lead them to me.

When we got to the coffee shop the man ordered two coffees, and with a slight smile on his face he lit a cigarette. There was something fundamentally irritating about this guy. Of course I would feel that way, in my situation, but even putting that aside, I doubted that I would enjoy his company.

"Uh, could I see your badge one more time?"

"Why? What for?"

"No, please forgive me but, it's just to be sure you're really a detective. At first, I wondered if you were a conman, or soliciting for something. Still, I never would have thought I'd be suspected of such things."

He had been smiling, but now he looked a little impatient. I had said that so as not to give him the upper hand, and I felt like it might have worked. He opened his badge to where his photo was, and held it out for me to see. I asked the waitress who was passing by for a pen and paper, and wrote down the man's name.

"Why are you doing that?"

"Oh, just in case, if anything happens. I'd hate if you were to take an unreasonable attitude."

". . . So that's how it is," he said with a slight frown, taking a drag on his cigarette. "Well, why don't we get started? I'm going to speak frankly now. No use talking in circles," he said, taking another drag.

I decided to look in the direction of the clock on the wall of the shop, with an uninterested expression.

"To begin with, we didn't retrieve a bullet from the cat. I wanted to see what your reaction would be, so I made it up. But there was indeed a report that gunshots were heard. The cat's body was found in a tragic state, and the eyewitness report about you—those parts were true. But we don't know that the cat was shot with a gun. Unfortunately for us. The body has already been cremated by the shelter, so there won't be any bullets coming from it. There's no way to know. As for the Arakawa murder, well, when an incident like that happens, we set up a task force, and even though the one for this case is extremely small-scale, well, we're investigating it as a homicide that's related to organized crime. And actually, we already have several people in custody. I'm in charge of that investigation."

"So what are you saying? I'm a student—this has absolutely nothing to do with me, does it?"

"Well, just listen," he said, taking a sip of the coffee

that the waitress had brought over. "You see, at first, I thought that this—the guy down by the Arakawa—I thought this case was a suicide. Of course, I happened to be the only one who thought so. The dead body, the way it was found . . . it struck me as unnatural for a homicide. Usually, gunshot murder victims are hit in the chest. Several shots to the chest. Well, most of the time. But this victim had one shot in the temple. A single bullet to the right temple. And, the guy died—well, the estimated time of death, anyway— between six and ten o'clock at night. By then it would already be dark around there. And what's more, you can be sure that none of those small-time yakuza thugs have the skill to strike with a single shot to the temple. No way. But the task force isn't stupid. Nope, and even if they were, they could figure that one out. Yup, this was absolutely a murder. The killer held a gun to the terrified victim's temple, and fired. That's what they think happened. Of course, it's certainly not an impossibility. Except these guys don't kill people like they do on TV. I've never seen a dead body like that one. Shootings, you know, by their nature, they create horrific crime scenes. They shoot the hell out of each other, without hitting the vital organs, and they die agonizing deaths. You can tell from the evidence, the scene shows that they were writhing in pain. It's never such a clean—well, it may be a strange thing to say but—such a clean crime scene. When someone is shot with a gun, they don't die right away. It takes a long time before they breathe their last."

The man had been watching me the entire time he was speaking. I had looked away, but still, his gaze made me anxious and there was nothing I could do about it. I was desperately trying to anticipate which direction his story would go next, and how it would be connected to me. Attempting to steady my fraying nerves, I drank my coffee and took a drag from my cigarette.

"There's one more thing I have my suspicions about. There was blood spatter on the fingers of the man's right hand. It was just trace amounts. Of course, it could have easily happened to get there. However, based on that, I had more or less decided that he had killed himself. Up to that point, it had been a hunch, but I could imagine him holding the gun in his right hand, pointing it at his temple. But once the police see any signs of organized crime, they are quick to make that connection. It's just force of habit. Especially in a small-time case like this one, with a small task force—it's all the more likely. But here's how I saw it. This guy committed suicide, and then by chance, someone happened to come by the scene—right? Totally by accident, they happened to come by the scene, probably someone who was just going about their business as usual, and they made off with the gun that was left lying there—that's what I think. The river runs between these two neighborhoods. I've been thinking that this person must be somewhere in one of these neighborhoods. And then, in the midst of all this, comes the report that gunshots were heard, along with the tragic discovery of the cat's body in the same area. It was obvious that someone had killed the cat. It occurred to me that, if someone had found the gun, they might first use it on an animal. I became convinced. I knew that I was right about this. I must confess, I was even a little excited about it."

He chuckled when he said this, and hearing the sudden sound of his laughter, I could feel a tremor deep within my body. I became aware that I was smoking cigarettes at a feverish pace, and realized that I was gulping down all of my coffee. Yet I couldn't help it. The man seemed to still be watching me, but since I wasn't looking at him, I wasn't really sure.

"And then there's the eyewitness testimony from that night. A young man—and I'd suspected that whoever found it would be a young man—this guy had been run-ning, a smile on his face and with his right hand in his pocket. On top of that, the cat's body was discovered in a nearby park at around the same time as the reported gunshots. This guy had been so stoic he didn't show a trace of disappointment when the gift to his parents was broken. Now he was running by, smiling with apparent excitement. Right? What do you think? It's not unrea-sonable that I would be so convinced, is it? I became interested. No, extremely interested."

When I looked at the man, he was indeed staring right at me. I was waiting for what was going to come next, but he didn't say anything. I pretended to look fed up, and with a half-amazed expression, I stubbed out my cigarette.

"That's just arbitrary guesswork, isn't it? Your own assumptions. This has gone far enough. You don't have even a shred of proof, do you? That's some nerve you've got, strong-arming me into coming here, when it's all conjecture, isn't it? Uh, may I go now? If you continue to harass me, it'll be me calling the police on you."

"Strong-arming you?" the man said, a smile on his face.

"That's right."

"But to solve a case you always start with guesswork."

"But don't you need evidence? In order to convince everyone. First of all, you don't even know whether the cat was shot with a gun, do you? You've just made up your mind that it was. And then that report of the gunshots, someone could have easily been mistaken—it doesn't prove anything. This is ridiculous. How can you suspect me like this, without any evidence? You must be crazy."

"No, it's just a general idea. All we need is conjecture. The evidence comes later. Anyway, we already have proof."

"What?"

"We have proof."

"So, please tell me what that might be."

"Your own attitude. That's right. You have the gun. I'm convinced of it."

He laughed to himself in amusement.

"At first, I had imagined the person might be one of those shut-in types, like a *hikikomori*. Usually it's those recluses who are really into guns, or so I thought. But you're different. You care about what you wear. According to the clerk at the convenience store, you're extremely polite, and you have lady friends—more than just one, even. And then—as I can tell from this very conversation—you assert yourself clearly. The way you tried to psych me out is impressive, but honestly, I think it just gives you away even more. Like someone who'd do something as stupid as killing a cat in a park. To tell you the truth—this will probably make you angry when I tell you—when I first went to your place, it was only to confirm what I already knew. I told you I had been convinced for a long time, but the fact is, I didn't want to regret it later—my way of doing things is to take care of every last detail that bothers me. Of course, I had thought that someone had the gun, but I wasn't sure that my deductions about you were entirely correct. As you so kindly pointed out, there were several flaws in my argument."

"Can I go yet?"

"No, wait a minute. But you know, you were extremely eager to hear about this case. You acted as if you weren't interested, when all the while you really wanted to hear what I had to say. And when I told you I was a detective, that caught you off guard, didn't it? You were totally flustered. I mean, sure, anyone would be upset to have the police at your door. But you were trying to hide your reaction. If you've done nothing wrong, there's no need to hide your shock, is there? My first impression of you didn't fit with what I expected, but since I've been talking to you like this, now I can believe that you would do something as daring as shoot a cat in a park. Call it a hunch, or maybe it's just experience—whatever. But I've really hit the nail on the head with this one. You're a strange one, all over the place. You must have shot that cat in the heat of the moment, huh? Even now, everything you say is so theoretical. But that stance, too—something about it seems superficial, just a bluff."

Again, he laughed to himself as he said this, which only served to irritate me.

"But, you have no proof, do you? You can't call any of that evidence."

"That's true, I must admit. I don't have a single piece of evidence. Or should I say, evidence is difficult to come by, under these conditions. All you've been talking about for a while now is proof. It's the guilty ones who are so interested in hearing about proof."

The waitress approached and cleared away my coffee cup. She saw the ashtray overflowing with cigarette butts, and went to replace it with a fresh one. Almost all of the cigarette butts in the ashtray were mine. Without asking my opinion, the detective ordered two more coffees.

"The Arakawa investigation will probably be suspended. First of all, because it's a suicide. And the people who are in custody, they will either be released for lack of evidence, or just rearrested for some other crime. If we're lucky, we might even find out about another drug route. But now the problem is the gun you have. My theory is somewhat extreme, as you pointed out, so my boss won't pay it too much mind. And the gunshot report, also like you say, they'll probably assume it was a mistake. It was the only report that came in, and anyway, the casualty is gone. There's no way to search for a bullet. You know, bullets actually travel pretty far. Even if it went through the cat's body, it could still have gone pretty far. To search for it, we'd need to stop traffic in the area and send out a bunch of officers. All of that takes a long time too. For something very small. Or a stray dog could have swallowed it, a kid could have picked it up and taken it somewhere—that would be the end of it. But I already have my sights on you. Unfortunately for you, I'm watching. It's unlikely that we'll find any evidence, so there won't be a large-scale investigation, but I can't just let it go. This is off the subject, but being a detective is a very demanding job. My life is busier than you can imagine. That's why, really, the easiest thing for me would be to wait for you to give yourself away, but it's too late for that. If there are bullets left—maybe one or two, at this point?—what comes next after shooting a cat is shooting a person. You will give yourself away when you shoot a person. And when that happens it will be too late. I have to do something before then. Am I right? It stands to reason that you are thinking about shooting a person next."

"I beg your pardon?" My voice shook a little.

"That's why you're thinking about shooting a person next, aren't you?"

He was looking at me when he said this, his expression the most serious it had been yet. I felt as if he had seen right through me, and I sensed my heart starting to race again.

"That's why I say this, for your sake—right now, please hand over the gun. If you don't want to do that, then get rid of it somewhere. If you shoot someone, we will definitely catch you. Here I am, right now—I will absolutely connect you to the murder, because the bullet will match the one from Arakawa. But, at any rate, you're not going to hand it over—no one wants to be arrested. That's why you should get rid of the gun as soon as possible. Someplace where nobody will find it. Like a garbage dumping area in a park. Take it apart, and throw it away with a bunch of other bits of junk. Do that, and that will be the end of it. You're still young. I have no intention of giving you advice, but there's no need to ruin everything just for a little fun, is there? Shoot someone and we'll get you. Please, keep that in mind. And, one more thing—I don't mean to lecture you about morality—but when you kill someone, they say that you lose your sense of reason. Of course, it depends on how you do it, but they say they have nightmares every night. You're still young. There's no need to do something terrible that will affect the rest of your life, just for the sake of it, is there . . . ? That's all I want to say, for now at least. Well, I'll be back."

I LEFT THE coffee shop, declining the detective's offer to walk with me, and went home alone. Even after I left the detective, my heartbeat raced with no sign of abating. I could barely think straight—all I knew was that I couldn't settle back down again. I returned to my apartment and lit a cigarette to try to relax. But maybe because I had already smoked too much, it just made me nauseous, and I actually vomited a little in the toilet.

13

I SPENT THE next several days mostly thinking about whether I really would get caught the next time I fired the gun. I hardly left the apartment, and stopped answering the phone. I didn't really sleep much either; I barely did anything other than polish the gun. I did so, quietly, the gun and me in my apartment.

I came to the conclusion that I would never be caught. Connecting me to the gun from the Arakawa case was a matter of speculation, and as long as that connection remained as vague as it was, I didn't think they would tie me to the another incident. For example, if someone died, even if they discovered a bullet in the body that was similar to the one found at Arakawa, they might be able to connect those two incidents, but they couldn't tie them to me. I figured I could get by, even if I were under suspicion, assuming no one could place me at the scene of the crime and, just to be on the safe side, afterward I stashed the gun someplace temporarily. I had the feeling there might be flaws in this thought process, but I decided to stick with it anyway. This made me feel liberated, which made me feel better. But at the same time, this also led to a chronic nervousness.

One thing I could not get out of my mind—what kept repeating over and over—was that if I didn't keep my wits about me, these thoughts would just spin out endlessly. Once I realized this, I was badly shaken up. The silver-black of the gun shone, its metallic luster penetrating deep within my vision, beseeching me. Or, I felt as though it were beseeching me. The woman next door was screaming, and I could hear something bumping against the wall randomly, accompanied by short cries. I tried to distract myself by putting on some music, but somehow, even as I did so, I was still trying to hear what was going on over there.

Yuko Yoshikawa called at one point. Actually, she may have called more than once, I couldn't really be sure. I just happened to be near the phone, so that was the only call I answered. For some reason, she was extremely worried. She went on and on—Why couldn't she get in touch with me, and why hadn't I contacted her? And then she just started crying. I felt as though I had been saved—I suggested we meet up now, and I told her I would come over to her place. I took a shower, got dressed, and went out. It was bitterly cold. I bought a can of hot coffee.

As soon as I was inside her apartment, I took off my coat and drew close to Yuko. "I've liked you for a long time," I said, caressing her face with both hands. Maybe she was surprised—she stared at me with a strange expression and repeated, "What are you saying?" I told her, "I really like you, and I can't stand it any longer." I brought my mouth to her lips, but for some reason she tried to avoid me. I told her again, "I've really liked you for a long time," and I tried to push her down onto the bed that was right there. But she resisted fiercely and managed to shove me away. I was quite surprised by how much force she used. She looked at me and asked, "Why are you smiling?" I didn't know what she meant, so I didn't say anything. But she asked me again, "What are you smiling about?" She gave me an insistent look, then seemed about to burst into tears. I was sweating, but I doubted that I had been smiling. So I left her apartment. It was still just as cold outside, so I bought a can of hot coffee, just like I had on the way over.

I DID NOT try to dissuade myself from shooting a person. It felt as if it were a matter that already decisively existed in my immediate future. Why the matter had already been decided, I didn't really understand myself. I was free, and was supposed to be able to control my own actions. I was able to do the things I wanted to do, and not do what I didn't want to do. However, I could not stop myself from thinking about shooting someone.

The gun was a man-made device, so it stood to reason that it had a purpose and, to stretch the point, a philosophy and an ideology. Musical instruments were created to play sounds, lighters were a simple way to spark a flame. A gun had been made to shoot a person—it was created to make it easier to kill someone. The general impression that people had of a gun, ultimately, was of death and murder. Being in possession of the gun, I was not immune from such associations, and imagining myself shooting someone was an inevitable progression. But for me to actually carry out such an act required negotiating that choice. Although the concept of killing a person was inherent within the gun itself, I had been able to ignore it, and I should have continued to enjoy the feel and the experience of the gun, as I had before. However, the gun burgeoned within me, until it took over all of me, a process that I had willingly tolerated. Even though I probably felt an emotion akin to love for the gun, there were times when, inexplicably, I felt as though the gun hated me—I was under this illusion despite the fact that the gun was an inanimate object. The result of such thinking was that I wondered whether I was ill-suited to the gun. I often felt that someone more cold-blooded, like you see in the movies, someone who coolly committed murder, who conformed with the ideology of the gun, would be better suited to it. The idea was extremely upsetting to me. At this late juncture, I had the feeling that perhaps I had discovered the sadness that one felt when, out of jealousy or despite your love for someone, the object of your desire turns their back on you. At times, I yearned for the gun to find favor with me, regardless of what might happen.

Nevertheless, I still did not see this ache for approval as a reason to shoot someone. Of course it was an influence—I could tell as much from the fact that I was even entertaining these ideas—but I still wasn't quite convinced, not even theoretically. This kind of thinking was not really my forte. Nor was I particularly good at analyzing myself; in fact, self-study actually inspired a feeling of revulsion. It took me quite a while to work through all this in my mind.

What distressed me the most was probably my own idea of what it meant to shoot someone. That option as a choice—as well as the images and sensations that I imagined went along with it—sought to connect with my real action, to move beyond the theoretical. I was unable to find the basis of that connection within myself. Whether it may have even been my own fundamental desire, I could not tell. Human consciousness is constantly shifting, influenced by various surrounding circumstances and instinctively fluid actions, societal norms, your perception of the outside world during childhood, experiences, the groups that you belong to, unconsciously accumulated information—it goes on and on, but this consciousness is an unstable thing, determined by the interaction of all these things—I knew I had read about it in a book somewhere. But I had to think. If I wanted to avoid shooting someone, these circuitous ideas were necessary.

In order to change the direction of my thinking, I tried taking the opposite position: why shouldn't I shoot someone? It was difficult to come up with an answer. It was a well-known fact that the world was full of people who didn't deserve to live, myself included, and the existence of the death penalty was societally accepted—whatever that tells you about society. And, after all, the fact that guns existed was also accepted as a matter of course. Conveniently, there was a person living in the apartment next door to me who would be better off dead. At that moment, it felt as if my thoughts had taken on a concrete movement of their own. Naturally, I would lose my freedom if I were caught, but I just needed to figure out how not to get arrested.

Most importantly, the truth was that I felt as though the gun had brought me back to life. Since having the gun, that fulfilling—you might even say thrilling—progression, probably formed as the gun insinuated itself into my life, became something automatic, and by tracing this transformation, I felt a pleasure that shook my existence as well as gratitude, and to deny that meant denying everything about myself. I wanted to experience every aspect of the gun thoroughly, and to abandon the firing of it that now loomed before me would mean there would be nothing left to do but to relinquish the gun. That was an impossible option, one that I couldn't even fathom. Losing the gun would turn me into an empty shell of myself, and the prospect of carrying around that lifeless husk for the remaining years of my life seemed like endless torture. I had often heard it said that humans lived to achieve what they chose to do, and I believed that. Putting one's soul to the flame, in order to experience such fullness, was essential for humans, and I had no reason to think that I was an exception. Thoughts of how to avoid doing so had gotten in my own way. I no longer felt the need to contemplate it. If I continued to brood over it, I would become paralyzed. And if I couldn't do anything, I would lose whatever value there might be to living. With this realization, I decided to pursue the idea of how, specifically, I would fire the gun. At that moment, I felt decidedly more at ease.

14

I BEGAN TO shadow the woman from the apartment next door every so often, and I got to know the general pattern of her movements. She spent the daytime in her apartment, she worked nights at a kind of local bar; Saturday and Tuesday were her days off, but there were times when she worked on Tuesdays. She came home at five o'clock in the morning; sometimes she had a man with her, and when that happened, she made the kid go outside. She was around her late twenties, she was thin, her eyes slanted upward, her hair was dyed brown, most of her clothes were garish but, on her days off, she often wore the kind of brand name track suits that were trendy with people younger than her. One day while I was shadowing her, I remembered how, when I first imagined firing the gun, I had envisioned shooting a young woman. At that moment, it felt as though this was something that had been decided all along; I had the impression that I was following, very precisely, a process that was integral to the gun itself. The place where she worked was in Itabashi in Tokyo, but she often went to a supermarket on the edge of the neighboring prefecture to do her shopping. I took note of this, and actually went to the supermarket myself to determine its exact address, which I got from a receipt. The store was in fact located in Saitama prefecture. Realizing that it would fall under a different prefectural police jurisdiction, I hit upon the idea of shooting the woman on Saitama turf. It seemed like this might confuse the police somewhat. To make the connection between incidents involving a woman in Saitama and a man from Itabashi in Tokyo would take some time, I thought—maybe not long, but a while, anyway. Perhaps it was only trivial, but it seemed to be in my best interest to complicate things however I could for the police.

The woman often went to that supermarket on Thursday, or sometimes Tuesday, between eight and nine in the evening. At that hour, the area was already dark, so it seemed to me like the perfect time. I began to consider the act from various angles, carefully investigating the neighborhood around the store to determine the best place to shoot her, along with my own escape route. I bought a black jacket from a local shop, and hung it on a hanger in my apartment. The dark color would be less conspicuous at night, which was absolutely critical for what I was about to do. The jacket was one of those reversible types—it was white on the other side—which I also liked. After the deed, I thought it would be extremely useful to be able to turn it inside out as I made my getaway. When I purchased the jacket, I also bought a pair of black leather gloves. They weren't a practical necessity, but I paid good money for them, in order to add to the excitement.

I placed the leather gloves and the gun on the table, and I gazed at the reversible black jacket suspended on the hanger. I also had a small flashlight that was still packed in its cardboard box, one of the things my mother had bought for me when I passed the university's entrance exam and moved out. I had taken the flashlight out a few days earlier and lined it up on the table along with the rest. The reversible jacket, the leather gloves, the small flashlight, the gun—these four items constantly reminded me of the fact that I was a criminal. Sometimes I liked the way this made me feel, sometimes I didn't. Yet these shifts in mood, this ambivalent consciousness that could be swayed by whatever vague reasons did not matter much to me. This was a simple process that I needed to follow, and what was important was whether I would succeed.

THE TOAST GIRL called, and I yielded to temptation when she asked me to come over to her place. The truth was, I was more inclined to turn her down, but it felt almost like an automatic response when I agreed to go. I took a shower, smoked two cigarettes, and got dressed.

When I went outside, for some reason I felt slightly dizzy. After walking for a little while, I realized that all along I had been staring at the top of a utility pole far off in front of me. I took a puff on my cigarette, threw it on the ground, and lit a new one. Several of the people on the street eyed this repetitive behavior with suspicion as they walked past me. A bicycle that appeared out of nowhere completely startled me—I almost collapsed on the spot. For whatever reason, the agitation from being caught off guard like that made my mind go momentarily blank. Lately, at least, minor things often startled me. The phone ringing surprised me, or someone knocking on the door made me terribly nervous. Even when I was on the train, I scanned my surroundings, my eyes darting restlessly around me. This may have been an affectation, but I must have felt a need to check one thing or another. Looking out the train window in front of me, I waited patiently for the station where I would get off to be announced, as nervous as if I were threatened by something.

Once inside the girl's apartment, I pushed her down on the bed. For some reason, she laughed, and told me to hang on a minute. But it made no difference to me. I could wait a bit, or I could do whatever right then and there. I felt thirsty, so I opened the refrigerator and drank a Coca-Cola that was inside. After helping myself to it, I felt a little guilty and apologized to the girl. She said something to the effect that those kinds of things really didn't matter to her, but I didn't quite hear her. She kept talking, now with a more serious look on her face, asking me if there was something wrong. I don't know why, but I reacted to her words with irritation. Wanting to have sex, I pushed her down on the bed vigorously, took off her clothes, and ran my lips over her body. The girl laughed and said, "Guess I have no choice," and she let me have my way with her. Or perhaps I should say, I let her have her way with me. In the middle of things, my mind was somewhere else. Once I realized it, though, I couldn't remember what I had been thinking about. At the time, I had been toying with her sex, putting my fingers inside her. I didn't know how long I had been doing this for; I was staring vacantly at her sex as my fingers moved unconsciously. She was making sounds, her body repeatedly shuddering in short bursts. When I increased my efforts, the sounds she was making grew heavily, and I wondered if they could hear her next door. As she quivered with these convulsions, finally she said, "Enough already!" It made no difference to me, but I held down her torso, pinning her legs so she couldn't move them, and continued to move my fingers deep inside her. She kept shouting, "Stop!" and her husky voice reminded me of the black cat's cry from that night. I persisted in what I was doing, but eventually she struggled enough to shove me off her. I had the feeling that was going to happen all along, but somehow I was still surprised. She was breathing hard and sweating, and she called me a pervert. The word penetrated me, as if without resistance. Ridiculous as it may have seemed, it felt as though something about me had been defined for the first time. That seemed funny to me, so I chuckled a little. Then I left the girl's apartment.

AFTER THAT, I walked around the neighborhood on the edge of the prefecture where I had decided to shoot the gun, and scoped out the area from various angles. In front of the supermarket there was a wide road, and beside it there was a small restaurant and a convenience store; it would be extremely conspicuous to do anything around there. As I followed along a street that the woman often took, I looked for a more out-of-sight place, and the best spot where I could conceal myself. In the midst of it, I got annoyed, and on a sudden impulse I almost headed straight for her apartment to shoot her dead right then and there, but of course I didn't do that. I chain-smoked cigarettes as I walked, and reassured myself that there was really only one place to do it. It was the site of a demolished restaurant. Not quite demolished yet, the structure still remained; they were probably about to begin work on it, there was dirty white sheeting stretched over iron scaffolding, and the only thing visible from what was enclosed within was part of the top of the roof. The woman had passed by here many times. Nobody would see the shooting if it happened here, and it seemed like I could then make my escape by taking the street in front of the building, heading in the opposite direction from where she came. I looked at the construction placard, checking to make sure that this spot was indeed part of Saitama prefecture and not Tokyo. However, the start date of the construction was five days from now. I was totally stunned—the moment I saw this, I felt a dull and heavy jolt to my heart. A voice inside my head said, *There's no time*. I felt weak in the knees, and I was sweating. The woman passed along this street between eight and nine o'clock in the evening; I thought for a minute about whether they would be doing construction in the dark. I didn't have to think long—once they started construction, I figured the odds were good that there would be people around at any given hour. Not surprisingly, the details of the work procedure were not posted, and to inquire about them was too risky. Posted on the placard was the name of the real estate company that held the title, and the name of someone along with a bunch of numbers I didn't understand, and lettering for a condominium's construction. I was flustered but I felt like I had no choice. I considered the deadline of five days—the only time to do it was Tuesday, four days from now—Thursday would be too late. Realizing that next Tuesday I was going to kill someone, I attempted to reflect on why this was something I needed to do, but my mind felt weary, so I gave up. I decided to begin my preparations.

If that woman were dead, I thought, not that it mattered, but maybe that kid would be able to have a decent life. His father probably wasn't around, so he would end up with a relative, or in an orphanage, but in any case, I figured, wouldn't it be a hell of a lot better than to go on being beaten by that half-crazed woman? Just like it had worked out for me, that kid might be able to have a better life. He wouldn't have to pluck the claws off crawfish anymore, and he could take regular baths. They might even be able to fix his squint, and he would no longer be forced to imagine sexual scenes inappropriate for a child. With these thoughts passing through my mind, as if to justify myself, I forced a smile to cross my lips.

15

KEISUKE BROUGHT NAKANISHI over to my apartment. But they soon left, chatting for only a few minutes. I talked to them as usual, they seemed normal too, but after giving the excuse that they had to get to their part-time jobs, they had left right away. I thought something seemed weird, but since I wanted to be alone, it was just as well. I had the feeling that Keisuke was trying to talk to me about something, but it might have just been in my head. He was smiling the entire time, and as he left he said we should go out drinking soon.

I took out the gun and polished it carefully. There were rare occasions when when I looked at the gun and it frightened me. During one of those moments, I was completely startled to get a call from Yuko Yoshikawa. "Would you come meet me at the coffee shop in front of the station?" she asked me. I ended up just going straight there. My eyes darted restlessly at my surroundings, I felt like I was searching for something as I walked along, and halfway there, I felt nauseous for some reason. I figured it must have been from smoking too many cigarettes. Yuko was inside the coffee shop, drinking a black tea. She took one look at my face and said, "What's the matter?" I responded, "Nothing, really," thinking I must have looked drawn and haggard. She was silent for a moment, still staring at me.

A young couple sat at the table next to us; the girl was doing all the talking. Last night she had been at a Denny's until really late, hanging out with friends, she saw a guy she was friends with in junior high, it really brought back memories. The guy DJ'ed at a club in Ikebukuro every Saturday night, and tonight was Saturday, so they should go together, she kept nagging the guy sitting in front of her. The guy replied noncommittally, eyeing the passing waitress in her short skirt with her dyed brown hair, on her way to take my order. I asked for a coffee and lit a cigarette, looking at Yuko across from me. The guy next to me, angry with the girl, said, "It's just a bullshit act!" The girl was like, "That's not true!" She went on and on, he had been in New York, he came back to Japan after the terrorist attacks.

"Hey, listen—I want you to be honest with me," Yuko said, looking me straight in the eyes. "Right, I mean, well. You were just kidding around, weren't you? With me, I mean. Because I couldn't believe it, that you would do something like that. Seriously, because I half-thought you were messing with me, you know—I want you to tell me, if you were. So. Care to explain? I'm the kind of person who likes for things to be clear."

As she said this Yuko's eyes were still fixed on mine. She went on.

"You know, that was really awful, what you did. Honestly, I mean—are you listening to me? Don't you have anything to say? That you hate me now, or you changed your mind—whatever you have to say, just tell me."

For whatever reason, I felt an uncontrollable urge to tell her what I was about to do. It seemed absurd, but if I had had the gun with me, I think I might have laid it on the table right then. But if I were to tell her, I didn't think she would understand, and anyway, it wasn't the kind of thing that I could even explain to myself very well. And if I did tell her, she would probably decide that I was crazy, and try to stop me, and when she couldn't, then I bet she would report it to the police. And that would create a serious problem for me. I wasn't exactly sure what kind of problem, but I knew it would be bad. And maybe I really was crazy. Just then, inexplicably, I felt as though I wanted to burst into tears, and though I hadn't cried in many years, overcome with that emotion, I actually choked up. Obviously, I was not about to cry in a place like this. What I did, instead, was say to Yuko simply, "It's no big deal." But even I wasn't sure what wasn't such a big deal.

"Look, Nishikawa," Yuko said. It took me a moment to realize that was my name. "There's something strange about you. Something really strange. I have no idea what you're thinking. I mean, there was something about you from the start—I was worried—but you're being especially weird now. Look, what's the matter? Did something happen? Come on, say something."

"You don't know what I'm thinking?" I said.

"I have no idea."

"So what difference does that make?"

"What do you mean?"

"I mean, who really cares if you don't know what I'm thinking? What does that matter? What does anything really matter? I have no idea, I'm telling you, no fucking idea—if I die, if you die, if my father dies, if that guy dies, or doesn't die—what does it matter? None of it is a big deal. None of it, at all. What matters doesn't exist. But you know what? That's all right now. Anyway, if I . . . No, if I were to—it doesn't matter—if I were to . . ."

I stopped there, suddenly embarrassed. I wasn't sure what I was self-conscious about, but I felt as though I couldn't stand to be there any longer. Or rather, that's how I wanted to feel—I wasn't sure why, but I knew that I wanted to leave, so I just stood up. I put a thousand-yen note by the coffee shop's register, thanked the waitress, and I left.

While I was walking, my cell phone rang—it was Yuko. At that moment, it occurred to me to toss my phone somewhere, so I threw it in the direction of an open sewer. The phone made a little clank, rolling in a slide across the asphalt and falling into the gap. I went to have a cigarette, but then I remembered I had left them in the coffee shop. In an attempt to calm my frayed nerves, I let out a little yell.

16

THE NEXT TWO days passed by swiftly. During that time, I was unable to complete any sort of mental preparedness or readiness. I spent most of those two days watching television. The strange thing was, that whole time, I didn't even look at the gun once. Since I had found the gun, not a single day had passed when I didn't look at it. For that to go on for two days in a row was really . . . I don't know, quite exceptional. The doorbell rang a few times, but I completely ignored it.

On Tuesday, I slept until evening, and when I opened my eyes, I took a deep breath. I remembered how, in a scene from a television show or movie I had seen—I wasn't sure which one—a guy who was going to shoot someone that day, when he opened his eyes, he had taken a deep breath. I did that twice, and then I brushed my teeth more thoroughly than usual. For no particular reason, I brushed my teeth for about thirty minutes. I turned on the television, I put on some music, and before long seven o'clock had rolled around. It was dark outside my window, and the news had come on. I realized, at that point, that it was already past seven. I opened my bag, shoved the bare gun into my pocket, and put on the reversible black jacket. "Just kill her and get it over with," I repeated several times.

It was cold outside, uncomfortably so. On my way, I became aware that the gun was stuck in the pocket of my jeans, and I moved it to my jacket. I made the transfer nonchalantly, as I continued to walk along. It wasn't until afterward that I noticed there was no one else on the street around me. But I felt like it didn't really matter—I might have even walked along with the gun in my hand. Still, I left it in my pocket.

My hands were chilled from the cold. I put them both

in the pockets of my jacket to warm them up. *I wish I had some gloves*, I thought to myself, and then I remembered the leather gloves I had originally bought for this day. I also realized I had forgotten the flashlight. Fed up with myself, I considered going back to get them, but I didn't have the courage. I don't know why, but going back home would have taken a lot of courage. I kept going, headed for the construction site I had decided upon. The site was very close. This surprised me, and I was caught by a sudden feeling of desolation, seized with an urge to speak to someone. Looking at that big white sheeting, I realized that I was terrified of the building itself. I tried my best not to look at it as each step brought me closer and closer.

I made it to the parking lot, and then I tried to sneak into the area that was clad in that white. But the sheeting was tied up to the steel columns with cord, and I couldn't find a place where I might be able to get inside. Those thin plastic cords, tight and secure, seemed like they were rebuffing me. But of course, that was just an illusion. I scanned my surroundings, making sure there was no one around, and then I held the flame of my lighter to the cord. Something about the orange of the flame that appeared within the darkness was nostalgic to me. What flitted through my mind was the light from candles atop a birthday cake—maybe that's what I remembered. The cord warped, seemed to squirm, and then melted into shreds. I did that three times, then I raised the material at the gap it created and went inside. The structure of the restaurant was still there, but it was kind of creepy without any lights on. The restaurant seemed large and imposing, and I felt terribly small within it. I sat down on the few steps before the front door, and lit a cigarette. It would soon be eight o'clock.

Through the small gaps in between the scaffolding and the sheeting material, I could see what was on the other side, and I looked for the best position. After moving around from place to place, I decided that the best spot was right in the middle, facing the crosswalk. From here I could see straight ahead, even make out the face of whoever was walking in the pedestrian crossing that stretched out directly in front of me. The woman often passed through the crosswalk around this time. Or rather, almost anyone who walked along this street used this crosswalk. I could use the time while she was crossing the street to make sure who it was. And once she made her way across, just when she reached this side, she wouldn't be more than two meters away from me. I waited for her to arrive, peering through the gap. I readied the gun with bated breath.

But, just then, I realized something important. The woman did not necessarily always take this street, at this time. Whereas she came through here quite often, it was not a certainty that she would today. I was astonished that now was the first time I had thought of this. Most of all, I was extremely annoyed with myself. If I was just going to kill the woman, I might as well do it without hiding in a place like this. I asked myself, once again, what was I doing here? It had seemed like there was a plausible reason to fire the gun here, but at that moment, I could no longer recall what it was. I felt ridiculous, and suddenly thought about going back to my apartment. There, I figured, I could wait for her to return home, then ring her bell, and shoot her when she came to the door. That seemed like a sure way to kill her, and more importantly, I thought, it would be easy. I decided that's what I would do, if she did not show up. It was just past eight o'clock.

I found myself staring at the ground. For some reason, I couldn't stop looking at the grass that was growing there. As I wondered why, I realized that there was no significance to the fact that I was staring at the grass. I wanted to warm myself up. *It's bitterly cold here*, I thought. A scene from a television show I had watched the day before drifted through my mind, of a guy getting beaten up, and then, the image of the top of the utility pole I had seen at some point popped into my head. There was nothing special about this grass. Staring at it, I said out loud, "This grass is nothing special." Then I thought about how bitterly cold it was here, and that I wanted to get warm. I told myself that I was about to kill someone, but it felt as though someone I didn't know were committing this deed, far off in the distance. Rather than consciously thinking the words *kill someone*, it was as if they were ready and waiting, already arranged in my mind and repeating in an unstable cycle. My gaze remained fixed on the grass. I had no particular interest in staring at the grass but, how should I say, it would have taken a lot of courage to look away. "Kill someone, kill someone," I repeated out loud, like a kind of incantation. The gun felt heavy, hanging loosely from my right hand. I had relaxed somewhat, but the gun continued to assert its heft. I had the impression that the echo carrying the words *kill someone* was, I don't know, lulling me into idleness.

It was then, the moment when my gaze returned to look out from the sheeting, that I saw the figure of a woman from a distance. She was walking on the opposite side of the street, then she stopped, exactly at the pedestrian crossing where I was waiting. The crosswalk sign was red, and I knew that when it turned green, she would step into the crosswalk. Which meant that she would approach the spot where I was hiding. At that moment, I felt an unexpected spasm, as if my body had shrunk in on itself. That tremor struck a sharp pain at my core, a condensed pain that seemed in a split second to be focused from my whole body to my heart. I could scarcely breathe, as if I had forgotten how to, and I collapsed on the spot. I noticed I was trying to inhale even though my throat was closed and, for the first time I realized that, in order to breathe, I needed to open my throat. Consciously I did so and inhaled. I felt like an idiot. Trembling, I couldn't be sure but my awareness was in shambles, I didn't think I could concentrate. Trying to gather my wits, I used what was left of my consciousness to remind myself what I was about to do, and I decided, first and foremost, to aim the gun. Being careful not to let the tip of the gun stick out, I leveled the gun at that slight gap. By then I felt that I had regained my alertness. But I heard something, and the irksome noise reverberated within me. It was accompanied by a pain, and it took a little while for me to realize that it was the sound of my own heart. Because it was too loud to be my heart—the sound was strange and mechanical. The moment I thought, *I hope the light never changes*, it turned green. With a sort of gloomy look, the woman slowly stepped into the crosswalk, gradually coming closer. She was bundled up in a baggy red track suit, and with her right hand she pushed back her brown hair. *In just a few more seconds, this woman will be dead*, I thought. Then I focused my attention on the gun, and I cocked the hammer. The metallic clink echoed keenly in my head, like something cold and sharp. In an attempt to steady my trembling right hand, I grasped my right wrist firmly with my left hand. But then my left hand began to quiver in the same way— it was a problem. My heart thudded dully; I had the sensation that scraps of metal were mixed in with my blood, and the relentless sound sped up, constricting my breathing. Both my hands were covered with beads of moisture, and the trembling had not subsided. *Don't think about anything*, I told myself, over and over. *Just go ahead and pull the trigger, then whatever happens next*, I repeated, *after you pull the trigger, you can think about it*. The woman was about to reach the end of the crosswalk, where the distance between us was less than three meters. It was striking distance—that fact shot through my mind with an almost electric current. The impact was intense, a sort of fervid liquid spreading throughout my brain and seeming to saturate it, making a splattering sound. Just then, a black hole opened up in my mind. That blackness encroached upon the fragments of my mind that were left, like paint flung on a canvas. I felt as though I could see the traces it would leave with my own eyes. Yet, in the midst of all this, I remained focused—*Pull the trigger, pull it*. Just as the woman reached the end of the crosswalk, suddenly she stopped in her tracks, let out a sigh, and turned back to cross the street again. Seeing this, I could not fully grasp what had happened. I should have shot her, I thought, but I had the feeling that I had gone off somewhere else, and once again something within me convulsed. The woman, seeing the signal change back to red, stopped in the middle of the crosswalk and turned around once again, then stood with her back directly in front of me. She was not even two meters away. I realized that she was once again waiting for the light, and I felt myself slipping into something like disappointment, somewhere between the short distance I was from her and the length of time it took me to fire the gun. At that moment, I felt like I was right there. Only inches away from the reality of killing someone, and whatever would come after that. What I felt then was a densely concentrated fear, one that might shake my very being. What lay beyond was overwhelmingly larger than myself, like a deep, dark space that went on and on without any visible boundaries. Within it was a crushing sense of isolation. If I became a murderer, I knew the memory of killing someone would stay with me for the rest of my life. The people who up to now had been kind to me and whom I had spurned—whether I liked it or not, I doubted that their enticements would reach me in that place. But the gun demanded that I fire it soon. The gun was everything to me. I was meaningless without it—I felt a savage love toward it. And yet the gun was cold to me. It drove me mad to think that the gun did not care, not even if I were consumed by that darkness. *I'm not the one using the gun*, I thought. *The gun is using me*—I was nothing more than a part of the system that activated the gun. I was saddened to realize that I had been manipulated by the gun the entire time. I had been manipulated by something man-made all along; despite never having attached much importance to my own life, I had sacrificed it to the gun. Just then, I looked at the scene that surrounded the woman. The dirty crosswalk signal, the asphalt, these buildings, these people—I didn't know who they were or where they came from. But I felt an intense desire for the tiny shred of my own life, for the worthless time I had experienced so far. This feeling grew maddeningly strong, beyond the control of my own will, and I was overcome. And yet, not to pull the trigger felt cowardly somehow. There was no basis for it, but that was how I felt. What would happen after I killed her, I wondered. It was possible that, even if I did it, I could go on with my life as if nothing happened. In the history of the world, hundreds of millions of people must have been killed, directly or indirectly. Poverty killed people, just as the atomic bomb did, that was for sure, no matter what anyone said. But still, I could not pull the trigger. My consciousness faded, my vision dimmed, and the next thing I knew, I had tossed the gun aside. It didn't feel as though I had done that myself, but there the gun was, lying on the ground some distance away from me. For a while I just sat there, in a daze.

Then the thought occurred to me that I could no longer be with the gun. The idea crept into my mind uncannily, without any resistance. But then a grief, unlike anything I had ever felt before, seemed to well up. For a long time, I wept out loud. My sobbing was a strange mixture of relief and sadness. My tears wouldn't stop, and I sat there crying without pause. Then, as I gazed at the gun lying away from me, for some reason I thought of my father, who would soon die.

I lit a cigarette, and inhaled the smoke deeply. As it passed through my throat, so recently winded, it made me cough. Then, I thought of that woman, the one I had been so fixated on, the young woman whom I tried to kill and who had left me and run off somewhere, just like before.

17

MY LIFE CHANGED a little, day by day. It was strange, but I began to really savor my own existence. When I saw something, I was aware of the fact that I was looking at it, or when I was walking, I was conscious of actually moving my legs. I started to appreciate the details and, as Keisuke would say, I became more sociable than before, though it meant I was losing interest in girls. I thought a lot about the part of me that was inherited from my father, and I decided that it was completely worthless. I didn't really know much about heredity, but it seemed to me that, depending on who put it to use, it could evolve in any number of ways. I exercised a lot, going to the gym to sweat it out. I went to the university, and worked hard on writing papers so that I could graduate. However, this is not to say that I discovered the meaning of life or anything. I already knew there was no such thing. But . . . how should I put it? I wanted to relish my time here, while it lasted. It may have been a small thing, within the framework of life that surrounded me, but meanwhile, I decided to spend the rest of my days living.

But there was one thing I had to do. Get rid of the gun. In order to maintain my current state of mind, I needed to get rid of the gun. This was, undoubtedly, sad for me. I still loved the gun, and I felt like banishing that sentiment would take a long time. If I thought long and hard, there might have been a way to hold onto it, but I figured that the best thing was just to get rid of the gun without dwelling on it. I was trying to be satisfied with my current state of mind, and to be satisfied, I couldn't have the gun with me. Maybe because of my abiding or unresolved feelings, I decided to get rid of it somewhere far away.

I put on the leather gloves and, just in case, I wiped off any fingerprints that were on the gun. My plan was to submerge it in water somewhere so that no one would be able to use it, so I thought maybe I didn't have to worry about fingerprints, but I did it anyway. I decided to go to the mountains where I had originally planned to fire the gun, and dump it in a pond or river. There was no particular reason—that's just what I had decided to do. Or maybe I did want to keep the gun with me a little bit longer.

When I was leaving my apartment, I took one of the bullets out of the gun. I thought I would keep it as a sort of talisman. The bullet still had a golden sheen—it was beautiful. I made sure to put it in the pocket of my jeans, and thought maybe later I should buy an amulet to keep it in. As for the gun, I put it in the leather pouch. I figured it might be a good idea to dump the whole thing.

Outside, I could feel the sunshine. The balmy golden rays enveloped me completely, warming me all over. I lit a cigarette, enjoying this feeling in my body as I walked. The sensation was not at all unpleasant. In a little while, I thought, the light would turn orange. I thought of Yuko Yoshikawa, and I felt a pang of nostalgia Then it

occurred to me that maybe I should try to tell her everything. I doubted I would be able to explain it very well,
but if I could, I wanted another chance to be with her.
I had just been sitting around watching a romance on
television, so maybe that had something to do with it.

I got on the train, and took the seat all the way in the
corner. Sunlight streamed through the window, creating
a beautiful color seemingly refracted through the glass.
I thought more about Yuko, and my mood improved. I
looked out on each building and street that I could see
from the window. The gun, in the pocket of my jacket,
seemed to be unmistakably asserting its existence. There
was definitely a gun in there. And, in a short time, that
gun would be underwater somewhere.

Just then, I felt a little sorry for the gun. It was an
inanimate object, so I knew that wasn't an appropriate
emotion, but I felt something akin to sympathy for this
man-made thing that had been created for the sole purpose of killing people. It wasn't as if the gun had chosen
its own fate, to kill people. I felt an unexpected and
keen sense of loneliness. And I knew that it would take
a long time before this feeling was gone for good. But
I had already made up my mind to get rid of it. I told
myself I shouldn't be thinking about it.

The train got more crowded over time, and I was forced to squeeze myself into the corner. The guy next to me was in his fifties or so, he was filthy and dressed like a bum, and he was sitting with his legs spread wide, giving me even less room. I put up with it for a while, trying to think about something more pleasant. The very first thing that came to mind was Yuko. Her face was beautiful, and I wanted to talk with her. The next thing that came to mind was the gun. With its streamlined function, its deep silver tone, the gun still belonged to me. And then, unfortunately, my brain went muddy. A cell phone rang; it was the guy's next to me. His voice was loud, he was laughing to himself, at who knows what. I didn't let it bother me. I looked at him, and kept staring until he noticed. It took a while before he did, but he just laughed with a snort, not bothering to pay me any further attention. Right then and there, I decided that this guy was the scum of the earth. As he jabbered on the phone, he was chewing away on the gum in his mouth. Little by little, that smacking noise drove me to the edge. I snatched the guy's cell phone, and then it occurred to me to toss it aside, so I did just that. Momentarily surprised, he turned to look in my direction. I couldn't help but find this amusing. Then

I ordered him off the train, shouting, "Get out, you bother me!" Yet even as I said these words, my brain was muddy and, at times, I was confused by the situation. "What the hell?" the guy said. "Pick it up!" he ordered me. I was struck by a single thought: I took the gun out of the leather pouch and grabbed the guy by the hair. I shoved the gun into his mouth, which was hanging open in shock, and said, "I'll kill you." I thought it was a pretty good threat, and even if the passengers around us called the police, I decided I would say that I was just threatening him with a toy gun. Some of the other passengers screamed and tried to get away from us. Both of the guy's eyes were open wide, and his breathing was rough. His labored gasps dispersed his bad breath, and the stench of alcohol mingled with the sweet smell of the gum disgusted me. His hair, clutched in my left hand, was slippery with grease, and the nastiness of it triggered a convulsive chill in me. His mouth wriggled around the gun, and when I asked him what he was trying to say, he mumbled, "It's not real, is it?" My next move followed swiftly. I cocked the hammer and said, "Let's find out." I thought that move seemed like straight out of a movie. As if I were watching from a distance, I let my body take over. I pulled the trigger and, that instant, I heard a furious sound. A massive spray of red exploded outward, staining the gray suit of a man nearby. Silence fell; I didn't fully comprehend what had happened. There was no more resistance in the guy's neck, it felt hideously limp and was bent to the side at a strange angle. It must have been from the back of his head, a huge amount of red fluid still gushed like a fountain, staining all over the inside of the train. The bits of red flesh and the red liquid strewn everywhere made an otherworldly impression. I heard a woman scream, and when I realized that people were running and trying to get out of there—that's when I knew I had fired the gun. "This can't be," I was murmuring. "There's no way," I repeated. The only thing I knew was, I hadn't needed to pull the trigger. I hadn't needed to pull the trigger, it hadn't been necessary to do it. Another future could have existed, I thought to myself now. I felt as though my body were slipping, and I was seized by the urge, as if in a fit, to grab hold of something. It went dark, and I looked around as if to ask for help, but to those frightened people, I was no longer human. My entire body convulsed, and I realized the area around my chin had not stopped shaking violently. My vision grew more and more narrow, I needed to grab on to something, and I caught hold of the steel pole in front of me. But it was slippery, and my hands were stained red. I wanted this all to be over with. The only way I knew how to end it was to shoot myself in the head. I had to do it quickly. If I didn't do it quickly, the terror of something I had never done before might break me, might shatter my body into little pieces. The premonition itself was already so intense, it was wearing me away. I would have fired the gun, but there weren't any bullets left in it. I mustered the effort to remember where there was one bullet left, and I groped the pocket of my jeans. I managed to use my trembling hand to retrieve the bullet. Now I needed to load it into the gun. My mind was not communicating well with my hands, so this task took some time. Around me, the people trying to get away were panicked, sometimes looking back at me as they rushed toward the part of the train that connected with other cars. I felt the need to respond to their gaze and, inexplicably, I tried to produce a smile on my face. The bullet simply would not load into the gun. Like a prayer, I offered my whole being as I pleaded, "Please get in there." Then, as if I were speaking to someone, I said, "Just a little longer now." And I repeated, "That's odd, that's odd," as my trembling fingers grasped the tiny bullet.